"Woods has an excellent ear for dialogue and an
unerring sense of pacing."
—*Publishers Weekly* on *Reckless*

• • • • • • • • • • • •

"Energetic, outspoken . . . Amanda goes after her
story like a dog who has latched onto a dirty sock
for life . . . fast-paced, enjoyable reading."
—*Mystery Scene* on *Body and Soul*

• • • • • • • • • • • •

"Ms. Woods has really hit upon a winning ticket with
the feisty Amanda and her reluctant
partner Donelli."
—*Rave Reviews*

• • • • • • • • • • • •

"Twists, turns, and jeopardy to spare . . . a fun read."
—*Fort Lauderdale Times* on *Body and Soul*

• • • • • • • • • • • •

"Ms. Woods' writing style is excellent, her dialogue
and characterization command attention."
—*Mystery News*

• • • • • • • • • • • •

Also by Sherryl Woods

Stolen Moments
Body and Soul
Reckless

Sherryl Woods

Ties That Bind

WARNER BOOKS

A Time Warner Company

WARNER BOOKS EDITION

Copyright © 1991 by Sherryl Woods
All rights reserved.

Cover illustration by Mark Hess
Cover lettering by Carl Dellacroce
Cover design by Jackie Merri Meyer

Warner Books, Inc.
666 Fifth Avenue
New York, N.Y. 10103

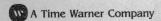 A Time Warner Company

Printed in the United States of America

First Printing: November, 1991

10 9 8 7 6 5 4 3 2 1

CHAPTER

One

*I*T was a muggy eighty-five degrees according to the Peach State Savings and Loan's neon green thermometer flashing cheerfully across the two-lane highway. It had been eighty-eight only moments before, outrageously hot for an April evening in Georgia. The distance from the church vestibule to the road was exactly fifty-seven steps, assuming one didn't trip over the weeds that grew in between the cracks in the sidewalk. Amanda Roberts knew all this because she had studied that thermometer and paced that distance once every ten minutes for the past hour, snagging her new high-heeled satin shoes twice.

Amanda's boss, *Inside Atlanta* Editor Oscar Cates, paced right alongside her, mopping his brow and trying with uncharacteristic tact to placate her. Her maid of honor, Jenny Lee Macon, trailed behind, along with photographer Larry Carter and the Reverend Seth Hawkins. They apparently had been rendered speechless by the

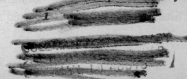

1

day's unexpected turn of events, which she supposed was a blessing. She wasn't sure she could bear an overt outpouring of sympathy. It was bad enough that the four of them exchanged worried glances whenever they thought her attention was distracted.

This was Amanda's wedding day and so far it was definitely not going according to her carefully scripted plan. She should have suspected things were going to spin out of control when the guest list had swelled from the ten or so people she had wanted for an intimate ceremony to nearly two hundred. Prospective groom Joe Donelli hadn't wanted to offend any of their neighbors, and that, apparently, included anyone in a seventy-five-mile radius. Invitations had gone to the mayor, the president of the chamber of commerce, and at least one hundred and fifty people Amanda could swear she'd never met before in her life. Just two nights before when they'd been counting up acceptances, she'd accused Donelli of sneaking an open invitation into the local weekly newspaper. Right now every one of those virtual strangers was sitting inside the sweltering chapel, waiting anxiously for the start of the ceremony or for the chance to gossip about the way Amanda had been stood up. By now enthusiastic bets were probably being placed on the latter.

In the last nerve-wracking half-hour Amanda had eaten enough jelly beans to fill an Easter basket. She'd grabbed them by the handful from her ever-present stash, barely noticing the indiscriminate mixing of ice-blue mint and tart lime, much less the unexpected sweetness of tangerine. Normally, she savored every burst of flavor. Normally, the gourmet candies soothed her, especially in times of crisis. Today, at the rate she was consuming them, they were more likely to lead to an overdose of sugar.

She had expected to be nervous. Pre-ceremony jitters were natural. When she'd married the first time, panic had set in halfway down the aisle. In retrospect she realized she should have listened to her instincts and run for her life. It would have saved her a lot of heartache in the long run. Not only had Mack Roberts dumped her for one of his sophomore college students practically within seconds of relocating her from her beloved New York to this godforsaken stretch of rural Georgia, but several months ago he had dragged her unwittingly into the middle of his lousy criminal scheme affecting some of the area's most cherished octogenarian matriarchs.

Donelli had seen her through all of that, proving beyond a doubt just how stalwart and caring he was. Even so, her instincts were again cautioning her. If Donelli did not appear in the parking lot of this quaint old Baptist chapel within the next ten minutes, she was going to take it as an omen and go on their honeymoon in Bermuda alone. She was nearly certain that ten days on a tropical beach would go a long way toward erasing the lousy ex-cop from her mind, if not from her heart.

She stomped back inside the vestibule and peered into the crowded candlelit chapel. The guests were definitely getting restless. Those cardboard fans with pictures of the Last Supper on them were fluttering like mad. At the whisper of the heavy oak door swinging open and then closed, heads swiveled and necks craned. The organ music instantly began to swell with the exuberant strains of the wedding march until organist Betsy Louise Dayton caught sight of Amanda's frown, faltered, and shifted into the chorus of "Rock of Ages." Again.

Miss Martha Wellington, her white hair perfectly coiffed, her petite frame clad in a flattering pale-pink silk suit, rose regally from her place of honor in the front pew. Using her best silver-handled cane for emphasis more than support, she tap-tapped her way hurriedly down the aisle, a take-charge gleam in her periwinkle blue eyes. Amanda considered sprinting into hiding, but knew there was no place from which she could escape Miss Martha's good intentions.

"Amanda, dear, you come with me right this minute. You're going to ruin that lovely dress if you don't get into the office where it's cool," she said, scowling at the Reverend Hawkins, whose round cheeks promptly turned an embarrassed pink. "Seth, what on earth's the matter with you? Can't you see the woman needs to get out of this heat before she faints dead away?"

"I tried," he said.

"He tried," Amanda concurred.

Miss Martha was unswayed. "Well, obviously not hard enough. Now, come along." The brisk tap of her cane set the pace as the entire group trailed inside the cramped excuse of an office, where an ancient window air conditioner wheezed in a futile attempt to combat the heat and humidity. Amanda waved a lace-edged hankie—

Jenny Lee's something borrowed—in a vain effort to stir up a breeze.

"Now, Amanda, stop your fretting," Miss Martha instructed as if it were a simple task. "Your young man will be here."

"In this lifetime?" she said, not wishing to point out that Miss Martha's judgment when it came to her young men was not exactly stellar. Miss Martha had adored Mack.

"Just stop it," the eighty-two-year-old matriarch of Gwinnett County chided. "I'm sure there's a perfectly logical explanation. Joseph is a sensible young man and any fool can see that he loves you. Now until he arrives, you settle down in here and rest. You don't want to be all mussed up and worn out for your wedding, do you?"

Amanda glared at her. She was in no mood to be fussed over. In fact, the more she thought about it, the more convinced she was that the ceremony should be called off. Any man who'd be late to his own wedding was definitely not a good bet.

She stopped pacing, planted her hands on her hips, and announced, "I'm leaving." To her chagrin, nobody seemed to take her seriously.

"Amanda, give the man a break," Oscar barked testily.

Amanda scowled. She might have known he'd take Donelli's side. They'd become pals, poker buddies, allies in the ongoing battle to understand women in general and Amanda in particular. He had been warning her for months to hang onto Donelli no matter what. He was convinced that no other man was capable of Donelli's infinite patience. In short, no other sane male was likely to put up with her tendency to fling herself into danger whenever she got caught up in a hot story.

Okay, so Oscar had a point. Amanda still wondered if getting married wasn't an extreme test of even Donelli's tolerance. Maybe they should have dated another five or ten years, instead of rushing into anything more permanent. That would have suited her just fine and she'd even suggested as much. Donelli, however, had been just as adamant as Oscar.

They'd already had several false starts in their relationship, he'd said.

This time it was either marriage or nothing, he'd said.

The former detective from Brooklyn might be patient, but he was also stubborn.

Amanda had almost made the trek down the aisle last fall, but then another breaking news story, the holidays, a winter cold, and another hot investigation had interceded. Donelli's patience had dimmed perceptibly. A few weeks ago Amanda had wisely stopped trying to offer rationalizations for waiting. Since she really did love him, she had decided to risk one more try at this marriage thing. She might not have been all that terrific at it the first time around, but she was at heart an optimist. This time couldn't possibly be worse than the disaster with Mack, and it could be considerably better.

Unfortunately, as it turned out, Donelli appeared to have had unexpected second thoughts. The ceremony had been scheduled for five o'clock sharp. According to Amanda's much studied watch, it was now seven minutes and twenty-two seconds after six. Even the very benevolent minister was beginning to look anxious. Local gossip reported that Seth Hawkins's tyrannical housekeeper always had dinner on the table precisely at six. If he wasn't there to eat it, it was just too bad. Judging from the slight paunch evident even under his loose-fitting off-the-rack suit, he was rarely late.

"Somebody do something," Amanda said, the plea as near to hysteria as she intended to allow herself to come.

"There's no phone in here. I'll go over to the rectory and call," photographer Larry Carter said, patting Amanda's hand. "I'm sure there's an explanation."

Since major rush-hour traffic jams lasted approximately ten minutes in this particular part of eastern Georgia unless the Bulldogs happened to have a game over in Athens, Amanda couldn't think of a single acceptable excuse.

"Larry, do you think we ought to check the hospitals? Maybe there's been an accident. You know what that car of his is like and the best man's not familiar with these narrow roads."

"Joe is."

"But nobody in his right mind would let him drive." Admittedly, she had a very low opinion of her fiancé's careful adherence to the posted speed limits. Every time she rode with him her jaw ached from gnashing her teeth.

She considered what she knew about Dave Michaels. He and Donelli had been friends since childhood. When Joe and Amanda had set the wedding date less than a month ago, Dave had enthusiastically agreed to fly into town to serve as best man. Amanda had met him only briefly before the bachelor party the night before. With his steady gaze, soft voice, and quiet demeanor, he'd seemed like a sensible man. A sensible man would have been behind the wheel. Ergo, Dave was driving.

Larry and Oscar exchanged nervous glances while Jenny Lee Macon moved into place beside Amanda and took up where Larry had left off, patting her hand encouragingly. No wonder the twenty-three-year-old *Inside Atlanta* receptionist and Larry got along so well.

"Don't you worry yourself, Amanda honey," she drawled sympathetically. "Larry'll find Joe and I'm sure he'll be just fine."

"Of course he will be," Miss Martha proclaimed.

"If he is, I'll kill him," Amanda muttered.

"Now, you know you don't mean that," Jenny Lee soothed as Larry and Seth headed toward the minister's residence next door. "Why, once he walks into that chapel all dressed up in his tuxedo and looking handsome as the dickens, you're going to forget all about this little delay."

Amanda turned a sour look on her. All that perkiness was sometimes very trying. "What makes you so sure he's not standing me up?"

"Amanda, the man has been pleading with you for months now to make a commitment," Oscar reminded her. "He's crazy about you."

"Then why isn't he here?"

"Maybe he had a flat tire. You said yourself that car of his is a wreck."

"That may be true, but don't let him hear you say it. You know how he feels about that disgusting old Chevy. He acts as if he bought it when he was twelve and tinkered with it until he was old enough to drive. It's like an extension of his personality. Besides, if he'd just had a flat tire, he could have called by now."

"There aren't a lot of pay phones on the back roads between his place and here. Maybe he's stranded. If Larry doesn't locate him, I'll take a drive over."

Amanda sank down onto the office's lone chair and sighed. Miss Martha stood beside her and fluttered a fan energetically.

"Exactly how long do you expect me to wait before we all admit that he's not coming?" she grumbled. "I hear it's a trend. Brides are being left at the altar all the time by these commitment-phobic men who get scared off at the last second."

"Now you stop that right this minute. Joe Donelli is one of the bravest men I know. He'll be here," Jenny Lee insisted loyally. "Larry'll be back any second now with some news. I'm just sure of it."

Amanda was not reassured.

"Do you realize that I spent nearly four hundred dollars on a dress I will never wear again?" she said, scowling at the silver-blue silk that draped and clung and shimmered in the office's dim light. Okay, so it matched her eyes. Maybe she did look more glamorous than usual in it, especially with her blonde hair swept up and capped by a matching hat with a provocative little veil that Jenny Lee assured her was just the thing, according to the latest bridal magazines. Who was here to see her? Not the man she'd bought the damned thing to impress.

And that wasn't all. She waved her bouquet at Oscar. "Do you realize that we have paid for the ballroom at that fancy, members-only country club of yours? You know how I feel about places that discriminate. It's a matter of principle. I still don't know how I let the two of you talk me into holding the reception there."

"Most of the politicians in town belong to that club. It ought to be good enough for you. Besides, the chef is the best one around these parts and you know it," Oscar retorted defensively, ignoring her comments on the club's restrictive nature entirely. As a journalist with a reasonably liberal code of ethics, he was caught in the uncomfortable position of having one foot in the New South and a whole heritage still living solidly in the past. His wife's family had joined the club generations back and nothing was about to uproot them or the majority of their upper-crust friends. Amanda didn't need to butt heads with Oscar often. He had enough trouble with his own conscience.

She scowled at him. "The chef is the *only* one around these parts, unless you count the cooks at McDonalds or Virginia over at the bakery. Not that it matters now. Dinner is probably ruined."

"Do you want me to call?" Oscar offered with far more patience than he generally displayed.

"Forget it. It's too late. The prime rib is probably shriveling up even as we speak. Maybe you ought to tell the guests to just go on over there. Tell the mayor he can use it as a campaign reception. The hors d'oeuvres alone ought to net him a few votes."

"There's still plenty of time for a lovely dinner," Miss Martha said.

"Maybe a quick snack from the McDonald's drive-through lane," Amanda countered, recognizing that she was taking out her foul humor on all the wrong people. It didn't stop her from continuing, though. "Another hour or so and we'll miss the flight to Bermuda, too. Nonrefundable tickets, of course. Donelli was so damn sure we'd never cancel out on our honeymoon."

"Exactly," Jenny Lee chirped, cheerfully ignoring the overall tenor of Amanda's complaining. "So, you see, there's no way he'll miss this wedding. He's just a little late."

Amanda glanced at her watch. "One hour, twenty-four minutes, and sixteen seconds. For a man who drives tractors and works out that's a hell of a long time to fix a flat. Don't forget the best man hasn't shown up either. Maybe they've gone off on the honeymoon together. One last bachelor fling. Maybe last night's party was more than Donelli could take. Maybe he suddenly realized that he'd never have another chance to sow his wild oats."

"I was there," Oscar reminded her. "That bachelor party was so sedate, even I was bored."

"Just because no naked girls jumped out of a cake doesn't mean it was dull."

"No cake," Oscar said in disgust. He was four weeks into a diet and beginning to get very testy about it. Larry and Donelli had voted against cake to keep temptation out of Oscar's reach. They'd figured his wife would keep an eye on him during the more lavish reception.

"What exactly did you do last night?" Amanda asked with a reporter's instinct for hot gossip and a fiancée's curiosity. Oscar and Larry seemed steady enough, so the bourbon couldn't have been flowing too freely.

"Nothing that will cause irreparable physical harm and nothing to land any of us in jail," Oscar confirmed, his tone flat with disappointment.

"Oh," she said, equally let down. A good juicy story she could hold over Donelli's head for the rest of his life might have distracted her from his absence and the passing of time.

The door opened and Oscar's wife crowded in. Curiosity was written all over the former debutante's still-unlined face. "What's going on?"

"No groom," Oscar said.

"Oh, dear."

"Exactly," Amanda replied. "I can't stand sitting around in here. I have to know what they found out." She slipped her shoes back on and stomped out, her entourage trailing after her. They were halfway across the lawn when the door of the chapel whooshed open and Mayor Delbert Reed came barreling out, his beeper buzzing insistently as he struggled to turn it off.

"Dang thing," he muttered, finally quieting it as Oscar intercepted him.

"What's going on?"

"An emergency. Don't know yet," he said and hurried on, an evasive action that was particularly surprising from a man who considered currying favor with the press to be his most effective campaign strategy.

Amanda was tempted to go after him. A good emergency with front-page potential was what she needed about now. Just then three more men tore out of the chapel, beepers buzzing frantically.

"Something weird's going on," Amanda said, falling prey to the local tendency to extraordinary understatement.

"Don't pay a bit of attention to them, dear," Miss Martha instructed. "Just a bunch of grown men with their toys. Next thing you know they'll all be carrying those cellular phones to church. Seth will have to put a stop to that before the services turn into chaos."

As she spoke, the minister and Larry reappeared. Amanda took one look at Larry's ashen complexion and this time she reached for Jenny Lee's hand. But instead of coming straight to her, Larry grabbed the pacing Oscar and dragged him aside. Amanda's instinct for disaster had been finely honed during years of chasing hot stories. Her heartbeat quickened. She took off after them, determined not to be left out of this one, especially when it might prove relevant to her future.

She stalked over and waved her bouquet of pale-peach roses and baby's breath at the two of them. Petals flew. "Okay, what have you found out? I can tell you're hiding something."

Both men avoided her gaze.

The last of Amanda's frayed patience snapped. "Dammit, Larry, if you don't say something in the next ten seconds, I'm going to smash every one of your camera lenses."

It was an effective threat. Larry's complexion lost the last of its color. Oscar's beefy arm went around her waist. "You might's well tell her, son. She's gonna have to hear it sooner or later, the way everyone's taking off around here."

"Okay," Larry began with obvious reluctance. He'd run his fingers through his hair so often that his cowlick was standing straight up. "I called Donelli's house, but there wasn't any answer. I figured that had to mean he was on his way, right? On the way back from the rectory, I stopped to get some extra film out of the car."

"Is this a play-by-play or what?" Amanda snapped. "Get to the point."

Larry stared at her, clearly hurt.

"Sorry," she apologized. "Go on and finish."

"I caught the tail end of something on the police radio. Not a lot. I was gonna make a couple of calls, try to find out more, but I came back to ask Oscar what he thought we ought to do."

"What did you hear, for heaven's sake? Half the men in town have just abandoned their wives. Unless word just came that the bass are biting, there's some sort of emergency. If there's a big story breaking and you need to go, go. Hell, maybe I should go too. A good armed robbery or murder might keep me from strangling Donelli."

Oscar's arm tightened perceptibly about her waist. Once more, Amanda was filled with an odd sense of dread. She was having an increasingly hard time ignoring the portents. This wasn't some random bit of news, not the protective, evasive way Oscar and Larry were acting.

Normally, the photographer was about as straightforward as anyone she knew and Oscar usually had the tact of a bulldozer. If they were tongue-tied now, it was for a very good reason. She had a feeling she wasn't going to like it.

"Larry, just spill it. What is it? An accident?"

He shook his head. "No."

She waited. He looked as if he wanted to be on assignment in some remote part of the world.

"Oh, what the hell," he mumbled finally. "I might's well just say it. A car bomb went off about an hour and a half ago not far from here."

Sickening visions of her own car exploding at dawn on a New York street several years earlier swam through Amanda's mind with exceptional clarity. The flash of light, the roar of sound were still astonishingly fresh. She'd escaped being in the car by just seconds. The horror of that memory, of being targeted for death by a corrupt New York judge and his criminal pals, still woke her in the middle of the night in a cold sweat. As a distraction, Larry's news was very effective. She couldn't think of a single reason why a car bomb would be set on a Saturday afternoon in this part of rural Georgia. The journalist in her, never far from the surface, went into action.

"Where did it happen? Do they know who did it? Was anyone killed? What was the motive? Is it tied to those bombings a couple of years back? Oscar, maybe we ought to get over there. There's a story here."

"I think maybe you'd better sit down, Amanda,"

Oscar said, trying to nudge her toward a nearby car. Apparently sensing disaster or responding to some subtle sign from the clearly shaken Larry, Jenny Lee hurried over and began patting her hand again. Miss Martha's grip on the silver handle of her cane tightened and her spine stiffened perceptibly. Even Seth Hawkins hovered closer, his expression compassionate. Pressure began to build in Amanda's chest.

"Larry?" she pleaded.

"Umm . . ." His voice faltered. "Oscar, please. Help me out here."

Oscar drew in a deep breath. "The car that blew up . . . was Donelli's."

CHAPTER

Two

"OH, my God," Amanda whispered, clutching Oscar's arm. Fear, its dark tendrils curling inside her, choked off her breath. An angry roar of sound exploded in her head. Again and again, the bright flash of light ricocheted through her mind. Metal flying. Glass shattering. Heat. It was all happening again, setting off a violent, familiar trembling.

With fierce determination, she fought the relentless waves of terror that could have immobilized her. Later. She would deal with the terror later. Now she had to act. She had to get to Joe. From years of battling such fear to do her job, she knew how to find professional calm in the midst of personal chaos. She closed her eyes against the threatened tears and drew in one, long, steadying breath. The horrible images and terrifying possibilities slowly receded. She squared her shoulders.

"Let's go," she said with quiet resolve.

"Amanda," Oscar said, his voice filled with a gruff, uncharacteristic sympathy that brought on the fresh sting of tears before she could muster the last of her defenses. "You don't want to be rushing over there just yet. Let Larry and me go along and see what's what. Jenny Lee can take you home and stay with you until we know more."

"Home? Not a chance. Joe needs me," she said, her fierce tone daring him to contradict her. "He must be devastated. You know how he felt about that beat-up old car. We were just talking about it. I have to help him find out who blew it up."

"The police will figure that out."

"These police?" she said skeptically. Her opinion of Sheriff Eldon Mason and Deputy Buford Ritter was well known. "Are we talking about the sheriff who gets lost unless his wife is in the car with him? Or maybe you have in mind the deputy, whose reading skills begin and end with the *Playboy* centerfold?"

Oscar frowned at the sarcasm, but for once he didn't offer his own more positive opinions about local law enforcement. "My guess is they won't be handling this on their own," he said gently. Too gently, considering the implications.

"Why not?" Amanda asked at once. "What haven't you told me?"

"What makes you think there's something more to tell?"

"Because you're being evasive. Besides, I know how

territorial Eldon gets. He'd only call for help if he was knee-deep in quicksand. So, how deep is it?''

Larry continued pacing up and down the sidewalk, avoiding the cracks, absolutely refusing to look her in the eye. She wanted to shake him.

''Dammit! Will one of you please say something?''

Oscar wiped a handkerchief across his damp forehead and stared at her helplessly. ''Jesus, Amanda.''

Her heart began to thud in a slow, painful rhythm. ''Please.''

Larry finally stopped in front of her. ''Amanda, there was someone in the car,'' he said bluntly, then looked devastated at having blurted it out. ''Oh, hell, I'm sorry. God, how could something like this happen?''

Amanda heard Miss Martha's gasp as if it came from very far away. She felt certain the whole earth swayed, rocking on its centuries-old axis. Only the unwavering brace of Oscar's arm kept her steady.

''No.'' She whispered the denial, but there was more desperation than conviction in it.

''I'm sorry,'' Larry said again, his eyes suddenly brimming with tears as her gaze locked on his. His freckles stood out sharply against his pale skin. With his brave facade stripped away, he looked like a kid struggling to understand the incomprehensible. ''God, Amanda, I am so sorry.''

The initial shock that had registered on Jenny Lee's face had given way to dismay. She was biting her lip so hard in order to hold back a sob that Amanda could see she'd drawn blood. Larry's arm went around her protectively.

"Joe?" she murmured, forcing herself to say his name, to insist on confirmation just the way she would for a story. It was a blasted instinct with her, even when she knew. *She knew.* Only something this horrible, something this deadly would have kept Donelli away from their wedding.

Larry's startled gaze shifted from Jenny Lee's pale, tear-streaked face to Amanda. "Who else?"

Who else? With a reporter's fanatical zeal for accuracy, she caught the faint inconclusiveness, the hint of uncertainty. She grabbed that tiny shred of hope and clung to it for dear life. "But you don't know that?" she demanded. "They didn't actually say it was Joe?"

Larry seemed shaken all over again by her vehemence. "No," he admitted slowly. "They didn't mention the victim's name. I just assumed . . . It was his car . . ."

"But they didn't say it, did they? Did they?"

Oscar shook his head, looking miserable. "Amanda, I hate this as much as you do, but you're grasping at straws. You've just got to be realistic. It was a powerful bomb blast. It was Donelli's car."

She whirled on him furiously, lashing out, her voice climbing with every word. "That's a fine attitude from a journalist. You don't have any facts. Would you go to press with that kind of supposition?" She poked her finger at him. "Would you? No. You'd have me checking my sources six ways to Sunday before you printed something like that. Good God, we're talking about somebody's life here. All we have so far is some flimsy little bit of information Larry picked up eavesdropping on the police radio. You remember that time Wiley listened to the police radio in the *Gazette* office? He told you Larry was dead, when what really happened was that he'd been hit on the head. That's obviously what happened this time, too. Larry just got it wrong."

Oscar blinked at her tirade. Larry squeezed her hand and said patiently, "Wiley is deaf, Amanda. He just misunderstood. I distinctly heard every word they were saying. Believe me, I wish I'd been wrong about this. Donelli was . . ."

"*Is*, dammit. He is! I don't care what you think you heard," she insisted stubbornly, yanking her hand free and heading for the parking lot behind the chapel. "The rest of you can stand around here grieving for Joe, if you want to, but I'm going over to get a few facts before I shed any more tears. Right now all we know for certain is that it was Joe's car. I hated that clunky old car and I'll be damned if I'll cry over that."

But she did. Tears clogged her throat and trickled down her cheeks. She kept remembering the way Donelli had looked when she'd finally agreed to marry him just a few weeks earlier. She kept hearing the emotion in his voice every time he'd whispered how much he loved her, how happy he was going to make her. And, God help her, she could feel the gentle, inflaming touch of his callused fingers against her skin. To never know that again . . . she wouldn't be able to bear it. She had to prove that it was all some terrible mistake. She had to see for herself that he was still alive, to know that they were still going to be together always, to remind him that together they would find the person responsible for this bomb blast. The reporter and the ex-cop. They were a team, an unbeatable team. Still. Always.

The next thing she knew she was running, running away from Oscar's sympathetic expression, Jenny Lee's tears, and Larry's doubts. She was already in the shadow-streaked parking lot before she realized that she didn't have any way of leaving. Jenny Lee and Larry had brought her to the chapel. They were still standing there indecisively in front of the church, staring after her, stung by her anger, bemused by her determined hope.

"If you two don't come on, I'll hot wire your damn car," she declared, drawing on the famed Amanda Roberts spunk that got her into trouble as often as it got her out. Right now it was the only strength she had, that and her faith that Donelli wouldn't dare die and leave her to manage alone.

Larry mustered up a faint smile at the threat. He shrugged at Jenny Lee, Oscar, and Miss Martha, then loped across the parking lot, put his cameras into the trunk, and climbed behind the wheel before she could wrench the passenger door open. Jenny Lee hurried after him and scrambled into the back seat.

"You watch how you drive," Oscar warned, still looking unconvinced and very worried. "I'll see you over there. Larry, you and Jenny Lee stick right by Amanda 'til I catch up with you."

"Perhaps I should come too," Seth Hawkins offered.

"No," Amanda snapped. She wouldn't have a virtual stranger muttering funeral prayers just yet.

"Thank you for offering, though," Jenny Lee said more quietly. "If you could just let the guests know what's happened, we'd be real appreciative."

"Of course. I'm very sorry for your loss. If there's anything more, anything at all," he said, but Amanda cut him off.

"I haven't lost anyone yet," she retorted, looking him square in the eye. "My fiancé is still alive. I will continue to believe that until I see for myself that it's not true."

"Of course, my dear. I just meant . . ." He bowed his head, then met her gaze and said quietly, "I will be praying for you."

"Come along, Seth, " Miss Martha said. "Let's not dilly-dally. There are things to be done. Amanda, I will be along momentarily."

"Really, Miss Martha, you don't need to bother."

Miss Martha looked indignant. "Maybe where you come from, friends don't pitch in at a time like this, but down here, we do. You remember that, girl."

"Yes, ma'am," she said meekly. The devil himself would have a tough time standing up to Miss Martha, once she got a bee in her bonnet, especially one related to Southern traditions and genteel manners. Right now Amanda didn't have the strength to fight her on it.

As Larry backed out of the parking place and turned the car toward Donelli's, it became tougher to ignore the

overwhelming sense of apprehension. "He's not dead,"
Amanda said adamantly, needing to hear the words spo-
ken aloud.

"Oh, Amanda, honey," Jenny Lee whispered, her
voice catching.

"He's not," she repeated, over and over, a litany of
hope.

It was only when they'd passed the roadside vegetable
stand that marked Donelli's property and were turning
down the dirt lane to his farmhouse fifteen endless
minutes later that she realized that she'd torn the petals
from every single flower in her bouquet.

Floodlights had been set up in Donelli's yard, illuminating the small white house and the splash of pink and
purple azaleas across the front. Police and curiosity
seekers were swarming all over the place. If they tram-
pled his brand-new tomato plants, there'd be hell to pay,
Amanda thought. Since Donelli had decided to retire as a
cop and become a farmer, those blasted tomatoes were all
that mattered to him. He was probably out there this very
second trying to save them from the lead-footed investigators.

Without a single thought about how incongruous she
looked in her fancy dress and high-heeled shoes, Amanda
jumped from the car the instant Larry braked to a stop.
She took off running straight toward the roped-off area,
frantically searching the crowd for some sign of Joe's
dark hair and broad shoulders. She spotted the mayor, the

chamber of commerce president, and several other wedding guests, but Joe was nowhere to be found. She turned toward the house. Sheriff Eldon Mason, red-haired and every bit as beefy as a bull ready for market, had planted himself solidly in her path. He always took some sort of perverse pleasure in symbolically standing between her and the news.

"Whoa, there, Ms. Roberts! Just where do you think you're going? This here's a police investigation. We don't need no hotshot reporters messing with the evidence." He pronounced it ev-i-dence.

Normally, she enjoyed lecturing him on the First Amendment rights of the media, but right now she was in no mood for it. Nor was she of a mind to exercise restraint in the presence of his serious attitude problem. "Let go of me, you idiot!" she said, aiming a fist at his belly. Oscar appeared just in time to stay the blow and probably keep her out of Eldon's single-cell jailhouse.

"Amanda," he warned in a low voice, his hand clamped firmly around her wrist. She wriggled loose and glared at both of them as Oscar said, "Okay, Eldon, what's the story here? What have you found out?"

The sheriff's dour expression brightened. He gave Oscar a hearty slap on the back. The good-old-boy network was alive and well in this neck of the woods. She should have known.

"Hey, bubba," he greeted Oscar, then nodded at the mayor, who'd appeared at his side, followed by half a dozen others still in their wedding attire. "How ya doing, Delbert? We got us a doozy this time. Somebody blew that car from here to kingdom come. Knocked the windows out of the whole downstairs when it went. We'll be from now 'til next Sunday hunting for all the pieces.''

Amanda's stomach began to churn as she peered past him and saw the truth in his claim. Bits of red metal were scattered in every direction. Whoever had set the bomb had intended to kill. She scanned the crowd again and again for some sign of Joe's dark hair. Oscar caught her desperate search.

"How's Donelli, Eldon?" he asked.

Amanda waited with her heart in her throat. Oscar had phrased the question carefully, but she knew that Eldon Mason, despite his personal respect for Donelli, would not make a similar attempt at sugarcoating. For all of his Atlanta PD experience and degree in criminology, the man had the sensitivity of a mud wrestler. Amanda wasn't sure she could handle one of his cheerfully graphic descriptions.

She had tried so damned hard to be strong, to hold it all together, to believe that this was all some horrible mistake. The scattered remains of Joe's car told her that the odds were against her. No one could have survived that blast. Her palms turned damp and the muscles across her shoulders knotted as she waited for Eldon's blunt response.

The sheriff shoved his hat back on his head and took the toothpick out of his mouth. "Well, now, that's the dangedest thing of all," he drawled with evident fascination. Amanda was sure he was getting some perverse satisfaction out of taunting her. She bit her tongue.

Finally, apparently realizing she wasn't going to snap at the bait, he said, "The flat-out truth of the matter is there ain't no sign of him."

Her held breath escaped in a long sigh. Relief roared through her, more profound than it had been on that morning in New York when she herself had escaped death. She reveled in the sensation, murmured a few heartfelt prayers. Donelli was okay. He might be missing, but at least he hadn't been in the car. Thank God.

Then came the questions, no longer a lover's frantic questions now, but a reporter's, cool and methodical. "What do you have so far? Who's out here investigating besides you?"

"Wait a minute, Sheriff," shouted Randall Begley, a slick reporter from one of Atlanta's television action news teams. "Let me get my cameraman set up over here."

The mayor looked pleased as punch at the possibility of television coverage. Chamber President Henry Lucas muscled his way through the crowd and stood shoulder to shoulder with the mayor. He blinked a little when he saw that Begley was black, but he stood his ground. Eldon, who was watching his chance to be in the spotlight disappear in a crowd of political publicity seekers, waved the reporter away. "I ain't about to hold no damned press conference."

Delbert Reed had no such reticence. He beamed at the reporter and waited for the camera light to blink on in readiness. "What Eldon means is that the investigation is still in its very early stages. He is on top of this and we expect to have a full statement before the end of the evening."

"Like hell," Eldon muttered. Begley pounced on the hint of dissension.

"You don't agree, Sheriff?"

"This ain't my investigation."

Amanda hadn't actually seen anyone from the Atlanta PD, but she wasn't surprised by the announcement. The mayor and his retinue of local leaders, however, seemed stunned.

"Who is in charge?" the reporter asked.

"Beats the hell out of me," Eldon admitted, seemingly bemused. He ticked off the candidates. "We've got the bomb squad from Atlanta. We've got some muckety-muck from the FBI. A bunch of 'em in fact. They were on the scene like locusts descending on a wheat field. They flat-out beat Buford and me over here."

This time he caught Amanda off guard. "The FBI? Why?"

"The Federal Bureau of Investigation didn't feel the need to enlighten me," he said sourly.

"We heard there was someone in the car," the reporter said. Amanda admired his tenacity in the face of a source who had just declared himself out of the information loop.

"Yep, that there was. Or leastways close enough to it to get himself killed deader than a doornail. The FBI described the guy to Buford. I never saw him myself. For all I know at this point it could have been the bomber himself, caught in his own trap."

Something about the statement seemed odd. "Is the body still here?" Amanda asked with considerably less trepidation than she would have five minutes earlier.

"Nope. Went off to the morgue about twenty minutes ago. Danged ambulance took off just as I pulled up."

"What did this man look like?"

"Hard to tell exactly, according to the Feds. He was messed up pretty bad. Blond hair, slender like. Seemed like he might have been wearing a tuxedo. Don't see many guys that duded up around these parts on a Saturday afternoon."

Of course, Amanda thought with a dawning sense of dismay. She looked at Oscar. "Dave Michaels," she mouthed silently.

"Sounds like it," he agreed.

The sheriff was apparently more astute than she'd ever been given any reason to believe. He pounced on the exchange every bit as aggressively as any reporter might have. "Well, I'll be," he said with obvious glee at his coup and no sense at all that he was still spilling his guts on camera. "You two know this guy?"

"Could be," Oscar said carefully. He glowered at the TV reporter. "Off the record, son. Shut that thing off." Only when the camera lens was tilted toward the ground did he finish. "If we're right—and I'm not sayin' we are without takin' a look at the body—he was supposed to be the best man in Amanda's wedding. Neither he or Donelli ever showed up at the chapel."

"Terrible thing," Henry Lucas proclaimed, turning his chamber of commerce smile on for the camera, which was rolling again. "Ms. Roberts, I'm sorry as the dickens about all this. Things like this just don't happen 'round here. You rest assured the entire community will not be satisfied until we have identified the person responsible. Isn't that right, Delbert?"

"Absolutely. We'll leave no stone unturned, no lead untraced," he vowed, unaware that the cameraman was already moving on to capture more dramatic shots.

"See that you don't," Oscar said, a warning glint in his eyes that Amanda had never seen before. She wondered if he and the mayor had locked horns in the past. She made a mental note to ask about that sometime when things had settled down again.

Right now, though, Eldon had other plans for Oscar. "You come with me," he said, tugging on his arm. "I'll take you over to the morgue myself. Whoo-ee, would I like to top these know-it-all federal dudes for once."

Oscar stared hard at Amanda. "You gonna be all right here?"

"I'll be fine. Jenny Lee and Larry are here if I need them."

Actually, from what Amanda could see, Jenny Lee was absorbed in her own investigation. Determined to impress Oscar with her resourcefulness, she appeared to be trying to sweet-talk the sheriff's deputy into letting her get closer to the remains of the car. If she succeeded and unearthed some unreleased bit of information integral to the story, she might yet win the promotion from receptionist to reporter that she so desperately wanted. Amanda left her to work on Buford.

She looked around for Larry. Predictably, he was snapping pictures, the whir of his automatic Nikon clear above the muffled exchanges among the search teams picking up evidence with rubber-gloved fingers, bagging each item and tagging it.

With the two of them fully occupied and unaware of what she was up to, Amanda decided to skirt the crowd and try to slip into the house. Maybe inside she would find some clue that would tell her what had happened to Donelli. A man with Donelli's raw courage and stubborn tenacity did not vanish into thin air unless he'd meant to.

Or unless someone had insisted on it. The thought was enough to make her blood run cold for the second time that evening.

C H A P T E R

Three

AMANDA slipped into the shadows beyond the floodlights and turned the corner of the house. She made it as far as the back door before three commanding male voices—all from different directions—rose in astonishing unison. One particular voice prevailed, probably because it was the only one not slowed down by a drawl.

"You! Where the hell do you think you're going?" a man who looked as if he ought to be running an accounting firm demanded, stepping outside and blocking her way. He'd apparently trained at the same police academy as Eldon, though he'd developed his sense of fashion from someplace decidedly more traditional. Eldon favored baseball caps and jeans, which interfered with her ability to take him seriously. This man exuded seriousness.

"Me?" she asked, all innocence as she surveyed his

bland gray suit, crisp white shirt, close-cropped hair, and scowling demeanor. ''I live here. Who are you?''

He ignored the question. Nor did he seem inclined to take her at her word. ''You have any proof?''

It was a tricky point. Actually, she didn't. Her driver's license still had her old address on it. An unsigned marriage license for a wedding that hadn't taken place probably wouldn't satisfy him.

''Well?'' he prodded.

''That's a bit of a problem,'' she began. ''You see, Mr. Donelli and I were supposed to get married today, only he never showed up at the church, probably because of this, so while we have been living here together, more or less, and were planning to be married by this time, I don't actually have anything showing that my name is Donelli or will be soon.'' Thoroughly out of breath, but pleased with the explanation, she smiled. He didn't.

''Sorry.''

''Come on,'' she cajoled. ''Give me a break here. This has been a very traumatic afternoon, as I'm sure you can imagine. I really need to get inside.''

''Sorry.''

The man apparently had a limited vocabulary, but he did seem to grasp the one word that would keep her from getting the information she wanted. As tired as she was, though, she couldn't rally her usual spirited defense of her rights. Just then Atlanta Homicide Detective Jim Harrison sauntered up, looking rumpled and weary and cynical as always. For once she was glad to see him.

''Tell him, Detective,'' she said, wondering which of

the three men in her path was in charge here. A quick glance at the third man's deferential step back told her his status, so she concentrated on the other two.

By her standards Harrison waited a beat too long before finally admitting, "She and Mr. Donelli were close friends."

It was a grudging admission considering that Harrison knew all about her relationship with Donelli. Together they had driven the detective crazy when he'd been investigating the murder of a popular Atlanta fitness instructor about a year ago. Only when they'd solved the case had he acknowledged a certain reluctant admiration for their intuition and skills, if not for what he deemed Amanda's reckless disregard for authority and Donelli's implicit tolerance of it.

"We were going to get married this afternoon," she corrected, figuring that might get her inside faster than some casual relationship.

The detective's wary expression altered at once to one of genuine sympathy. "God, I'm sorry, Amanda. I had not idea. Is Joe with you, then? Was he already at the church when this happened? We haven't been able to locate him."

She shook her head. "He never made it to the chapel."

"And you haven't heard from him?"

"Not a word."

The man in the gray suit, who'd been listening avidly, appeared disgusted by her lack of concrete knowledge of a key player in the case, especially when said player happened to be her own missing fiancé. After that brief flash of curiosity, it was plain he'd now lost interest. Even she had to admit that she'd lost a certain edge of credibility. Before he could vanish back inside, she asked quickly, "Now that Detective Harrison has vouched for me, surely it's okay if I come in and take a look around."

His expression hardened as if she'd expressed a desire to delve into state secrets. "Not a chance. We can't take the risk you'll tamper with the evidence." At his words, the third man moved back in front of the screen door, effectively blocking her access. Unless she wanted to get into a wrestling match with a guy who looked as if he sparred with heavyweight champions just for fun, she was going to have to talk her way inside or come back later and climb through a window. She wasn't sure she had the patience or the energy for the latter. She started talking.

"I know better than to touch anything," she reassured them. "I'm a reporter. I've been on crime scenes. Detective Harrison can vouch for me." She figured it was a toss-up whether he'd back her up or send her packing, but it was the only wedge she had.

"Sorry," the other man insisted without even glancing toward the Atlanta homicide detective. "You won't be on this one."

She opened her mouth to argue, but Detective Harrison guided her away. "Forget it, Amanda. You won't win. We'll get you in there soon enough," he promised when she started to mount another argument. "These by-the-book government types get hysterical at anybody getting on their turf. They've kept me pacing around out here for the last hour while they secured the scene.''

''He's FBI?''

''Yep. Agent Jeffrey Dunne.'' He grinned. ''You honestly couldn't tell? He'll be ecstatic. He worries a lot about his image.''

''Who called the FBI in? You?''

''Not me. I'm perfectly content to work my own cases.''

''Eldon?''

One eyebrow lifted skeptically. ''You can't be serious. He's been waiting for the day when he'd get something really big out here.''

''Then this guy Dunne just appeared?''

''Maybe he monitors the police band just for kicks.''

''I don't suppose you want to tell me what you have so far,'' she said, without much hope. The detective was usually far more inclined to drag information out of her than he was to reciprocate.

To her surprise, he admitted, ''I don't have a hell of a lot. Jeffrey Dunne was first on the scene. That makes him king of the hill. The rest of us have been cast in supporting roles.'' His disgruntlement and frustration were plain. ''What about you?''

''I'm just getting started. Oscar's gone to ID the victim. If we're right, it's a friend of Joe's from New York, Dave Michaels. He was going to be our best man. He just got into town last night. My guess is that Joe was the target and Dave just happened to get in the way. Everyone around here knew about the wedding. Anyone could have timed that bomb, knowing Joe would be leaving for the church about then.''

''But who would want to?''

''That's the part that doesn't make any sense. He's gotten to be a real part of the community. Nobody that I can think of has anything against him.''

''Has he been working cases lately? I heard he'd finally decided to get licensed as a private investigator.''

''He'd gone for the license, but as far as I know he was still caught up in battling terrorist aphids in his garden. I'm sure he would have mentioned it if he'd actually taken on a case. He knew how anxious I was for him to start investigating something more complex than blight.''

''But you don't know that for sure?''

She shook her head. ''The last couple of weeks I've been so caught up in planning for this last-minute wedding, getting my house on the market, and finishing up a piece for *Inside Atlanta,* it never occurred to me to ask. Besides, it was spring planting season. He considers that some sort of religious rite. All he talked about was getting all his seeds in the ground before we left on our honeymoon.''

''Did he seem distracted? Was he away from the house more than usual, especially considering what he had to do around here? Anything that might suggest he was conducting an investigation?''

She started to tell him no, then recalled a couple of phone calls that had seemed to upset Donelli. She'd asked about them, but his answers had been evasive.

She'd been too distracted herself to pursue it. She described the incidents to Detective Harrison.

"It could be connected. At this point, I'll grasp at any straw. If you're game, I have an idea. It goes against my grain, but so does leaving this entire investigation in Dunne's hands."

Amanda's spirits brightened at the prospect of action. "Let's go for it."

Instead of being pleased by her enthusiasm, the cautious Harrison regarded her ruefully. "You really do tend to leap before you look, don't you?"

"You're not the type to suggest breaking the law. I think it's a safe bet. Am I wrong?"

"Why do I hate admitting that you're not?" he grumbled, as if he wished he had a slightly more interesting and reckless reputation. He sighed. "Oh, well, never mind. If I can get you into the house, do you think you might be able to find any records Joe might have kept? Was he that organized?"

"See what I mean," she gloated. "That's a breeze. He kept detailed farm records. Even though cops traditionally hate paperwork, I can't imagine that he'd treat an investigation any less seriously. Won't the FBI be able to locate anything I could find, though?"

"Not necessarily. You know his habits. You might recognize the significance of some notation that they'd never even notice. You'll have to be quick, though. I doubt I can buy you much time."

Suddenly struck by his somber tone, she regarded him worriedly. His attitude confirmed her own growing sense that Joe's disappearance had very ominous overtones. "This goes beyond discovering who's behind the car bombing, doesn't it? You think that bomb was more than a warning. You believe it was meant to kill Joe and that he's still in danger."

"Don't you? Can you think of any other reason he wouldn't show up at your wedding?"

"Cold feet?"

"So he blew up his car and killed his best friend?"

She winced, surprised at how successfully she'd managed to block Dave's death and its implications from her mind. "Sorry. It was a bad joke. I've been trying to convince myself this was some terrible prank that went awry."

"This was no prank, Amanda. I really don't like the way this is adding up."

His increasingly serious demeanor was beginning to scare her all over again. "Why?"

"You'll see when you get inside. The house has been trashed pretty thoroughly. Whoever blew up that car stuck around to go through the place. Maybe he didn't realize that Joe had survived. Maybe they had a confrontation. Maybe not. All I know is he's missing and I have more questions than answers, including the fact that the FBI got here faster than a speeding bullet."

"You think he's been kidnapped," she said flatly, admitting the fear that had been playing nip and tuck with the less violent alternatives.

He nodded slowly. "It's a possibility."

"And the FBI involvement?"

"Maybe they got the ransom note. I don't know. It's another angle I just can't figure and I don't like things that don't make sense."

From what she'd seen of Jim Harrison in the past, he was not an alarmist. He was, however, a hardheaded realist. "And the other possibilities?" she asked.

He shook his head, his expression grave. "I think that's enough speculation for the moment."

As far as Amanda was concerned, that nonanswer spoke volumes. There was no more time to waste. "Get me inside."

Without another word, he led her to the back door. Jeffrey Dunne's colleague was still stationed firmly in their way. He nodded at Detective Harrison and ignored Amanda altogether.

"My orders are that no one comes in, sir."

"Ms. Roberts just needs to pick up a few personal items. You can stick with us, if you like."

The young man hesitated, then said, "That might be okay. Wait here. I'll go check."

As soon as he'd gone, the detective nodded at her. "You should have about two minutes of freedom and maybe another ten after that with him watching over your shoulder. It's not much. I'll do what I can to slow them down."

"I'll make it enough," she said and headed straight for the den, where Joe kept all of his files. She went straight to the drawer where he would have been most likely to place his PI license. It was also the logical place for any case files. There were half a dozen unlabeled and empty folders. The top of the desk was littered with papers from the remaining drawers. She sifted through those as quickly as she could, but saw nothing beyond receipts for seeds and fertilizer and a repair bill for the tractor. She couldn't find a license or any cryptic notes.

She was on her knees gathering up the papers on the floor when a furious Jeffrey Dunne came charging in. "Ms. Roberts!"

Judging him to be a man who would be uneasy with emotion, she lifted her gaze, her lower lip trembling. Her distress was only partially feigned. "I can't leave it like this," she protested.

He immediately looked uncomfortable. "I'm afraid you'll have to, at least for the time being. I'll have to ask you to leave."

There was a faint note of regret in his voice. She decided it was as much of an opening as she was likely to get. "At least let me get a few things from the bedroom," she improvised.

He appeared torn.

"Come on, Dunne," Detective Harrison said. "Give the woman a break. She might even see something up there that could help with the investigation."

"Okay, okay, but I'll come with you." He glowered fiercely at the detective. "I'll deal with you later, Harrison."

"I can hardly wait."

Biting her lip to stop a very real onset of tears, Amanda walked through the ransacked house to the bedroom. A suitcase that had been packed for their honeymoon was open on the bed, the contents strewn everywhere. She picked up the delicate silk and lace negligee and a few other personal items with the FBI agent leaning against the doorjamb and observing every move.

"I assume you don't have any further need for these," she said stiffly. He responded with a scowl.

She stuffed the items into the suitcase, then said, "I need my tape recorder. It's in the guest room."

"Get it," he said tersely.

Inside that room, she surveyed the damage and tried to hide her shock. She found the tape recorder on top of the dresser where she'd left it, but the cassettes had been broken open and the tapes removed. The now-useless brown ribbons streamed over everything. She did the best she could to visually inventory the rest of the room's contents before Dunne hustled her out the door.

"How soon can I move back in?" she asked.

"I'd like to keep the scene secured until the evidence team has gone over it thoroughly. Couldn't you stay with a friend for a few days? If not, we'll put you up in a hotel."

"I could stay in my own house for a few days. I haven't sold it yet. But I want to be here." He chin jutted up. Her eyes locked with his. "I *need* to be here."

Dunne was the first to look away. He nodded. "Okay, then. Probably sometime late tomorrow."

"Thank you."

"Ms. Roberts," he said and this time his voice was almost gentle.

"Yes?"

"We're on the same side here."

She drew in a deep breath and nodded. "I suppose so," she said cautiously. Deep in her gut, she had her doubts, though. Maybe it was all those rebellious, antiestablishment protests she'd participated in as a college student years ago. Maybe it was all the stories she'd investigated on the corruption of public officials.

More likely, it was the fact that the guest room no longer contained the slightest evidence that Dave Michaels had ever been there.

CHAPTER

Four

WHEN Larry and Jenny Lee finally found her, Amanda was huddled in a lawn chair, still clutching the suitcase filled with her trousseau and the tape recorder, her thoughts racing a mile a minute.

"Amanda, honey, you're going to catch your death of cold out here," Jenny Lee fussed. "The temperature's dropped way down since dusk. You should have stayed inside or gotten a sweater. You're lucky Miss Martha didn't catch you. She would have pitched a fit."

"I was lucky they let me in at all. I didn't have time to gather up a fashionable ensemble. Where is Miss Martha now, by the way?" She glanced around nervously.

"I talked her into going home," Larry said. "I promised her that Jenny Lee and I would see that you got a healthy dinner and a good night's sleep. She was making

noises about settling you in at her place and having Della
fix you up some broth.''

Amanda shuddered at the very thought of all that
hovering. "Bless you.''

"Don't thank me yet. She'll be back in the morning,
I'm sure.''

"By then, I'll have the strength to do battle with her.''
She turned to Jenny Lee. "What did you find out? I saw
you talking to Eldon's deputy.''

"First off, Buford seems to think this was pretty
amateurish.''

"And what exactly does Buford know about bombs?''
Amanda inquired with a sort of knee-jerk derisiveness
she thought she'd finally gotten past, thanks to Donelli's
oft-repeated lectures on the subject. Apparently, this car
bombing and murder were going to bring out the worst of
her prejudices. Donelli would not be pleased.

"He was an expert in plastic explosives in the Marines
back in Vietnam,'' Jenny Lee said, a hint of censure in
her voice. Amanda often forgot that Jenny Lee had been
raised around here and wasn't nearly as scornful of the
overall mentality of the police as she tended to be.
Occasionally, her more open mind netted solid information. This appeared to be one of those times.

"I'm sorry,'' Amanda apologized, genuinely contrite.
"What did he say?''

"That an expert would have used a lot less and
probably something more sophisticated. This was just a
bunch of old dynamite with a timing device. He said he
couldn't get a real good look at the scene because of the

FBI and all, but he'd guess that the materials could be gotten just about anywhere. He says there's some road work going on over in the next county. He's gonna check to see if it could have come from that. He promised to call me the minute he finds anything.''

"Has anyone seen Donelli all day?''

"Nobody I talked to, except for Virginia. She came by on her way home from church and said he and Dave had stopped by the bakery for blueberry pancakes this morning. She looked real shook up when she saw the car. You know that expression folks get when something scares the dickens out of them, but they still can't turn away, well, that's just the way she looked. I know just how she felt. It gave me goose bumps, when I thought of how it could have been Joe, just as easily as his friend.''

Amanda understood, too. It was something she didn't want to dwell on either. She turned to Larry. "Did you pick up anything while you were shooting pictures?''

"I had enough trouble just getting close enough to shoot anything. They've roped off half the damn property. I finally got my long lens. Maybe when I do the prints, we'll be able to see something. Any idea what we're looking for?''

"No, not really. Are you going over to the darkroom tonight?''

"It's late. Oscar won't need the prints right away. Tomorrow morning will be soon enough. I thought I'd take you two home.''

"I want to see them tonight,'' Amanda insisted. "We can't waste a minute if we're going to find Joe.''

"Amanda, honey, you need to get some rest," Jenny Lee said. "You come on home with me. It won't help Joe a bit if you make yourself sick. Larry will bring the prints over first thing in the morning. We're all dead on our feet."

Amanda finally conceded that just because she was wound up tight didn't mean that she had the right to put more pressure on Larry and Jenny Lee. They did look exhausted. "Look," she said, "I won't be able to sleep, but if you all are tired, go on home. I'll stick around here in case Oscar comes back with news from the morgue. If it was Dave Michaels who was killed, I probably ought to be the one to call his wife, if they haven't called already. I think Joe would want me to do that."

Suddenly, the tension and uncertainty were too much for her. At the image of the sweet, gentle man she'd met the night before lying dead now, all of the tears she'd held at bay spilled down her cheeks. Instantly angry at the loss of control, she brushed them away. "Damn, I am not going to start crying now. Falling apart won't help anything. I need to keep my wits about me if I'm going to help Joe."

"It's okay, Amanda. If anybody's got a right to be upset, you do," Larry said. "This is hardly the way the day was supposed to turn out."

"Hey, Donelli promised me a wedding to remember," she said with sheer bravado. "He sure as hell delivered on that, didn't he?"

Jenny Lee glared at Larry. "If the time ever comes

when you and I get married, just remember one thing, Larry Carter. I'll be perfectly happy with something a little more traditional.''

''I'll keep that in mind,'' Larry vowed and for the first time all night, Amanda found herself smiling. It was reassuring to see that in the midst of chaos, some things never changed. Since the day they'd met, Jenny Lee hadn't missed an opportunity to nudge the determinedly single photographer straight toward an altar. It appeared Larry just might be becoming resigned to his fate.

Before she could send the two of them off to debate their own future wedding plans, Delbert Reed, Henry Lucas, and several other local politicians came up.

''Ms. Roberts, I just want you to know that we're calling a town meeting for tomorrow night to get to the bottom of this,'' the mayor said. ''We all like Joe and we want to see to it that whoever's behind this little incident is brought to justice.''

Little incident? Amanda stared at him incredulously. That was somewhat like calling the Persian Gulf War a minor glitch in Middle East relations. ''How do you expect to accomplish that?'' she asked curiously.

''I do think if we all put our heads together we can come up with a plan,'' Henry Lucas said. She noticed he didn't mention anything as mundane as evidence.

''Will Jeffrey Dunne be there?''

''Who's he?'' Lucas asked.

''The FBI agent in charge of the investigation.''

The chamber president looked nervously toward Delbert Reed. "I don't expect so," the mayor admitted.

"How about Detective Harrison?"

"This is a local matter, Ms. Roberts," he said. "The sheriff will be there. Can we expect you?"

"I wouldn't miss it for the world." With any luck it would be her first chance to see an old-fashioned lynch mob in action.

Whatever else he might be . . . and Amanda was beginning to form some definite, derogatory ideas about that . . . at least Jeffrey Dunne was true to his promise. At four o'clock the following afternoon, he sent word to Jenny Lee's via one of his loyal minions that Amanda could move back into Donelli's house. Jenny Lee passed along the message with obvious reluctance.

"Amanda, honey, I don't think you ought to be moving back in there," she said, her forehead puckered with a worried frown.

"For a woman who is nearly ten years younger than I am, you have an amazing capacity for acting like my mother," Amanda grumbled. "There is no reason not to stay there."

Miss Martha, who'd arrived just in time to hear the message, chimed right in. "Well, I happen to agree with Jenny Lee. If anything, you should come to stay with me. I have plenty of room to spare in that big old house and Della and I can look after you until all of this is settled. You know your parents would rest better if they knew you were safe.''

As it had the night before, the prospect of all that well-meant nurturing made Amanda shudder. ''I really do not need looking after,'' she said very firmly. ''And my parents know nothing about this. I don't intend to call them until we have some answers.''

Miss Martha's eyes widened with shock. ''My dear, you must call. They would want to know. I realize they couldn't travel all this way just now because of your father's health, but surely you don't intend to let them think your wedding went off without a hitch.''

''That's exactly what I intend. I won't risk my father having another heart attack worrying about me.''

''And what about the rest of us?'' Jenny Lee grumbled. ''You don't think we'll worry? You should have heard Oscar earlier, when I told him you were thinking about going back there.''

Amanda blushed guiltily. ''It's not the same.''

''Oh, isn't it?'' she contradicted. She held up a perfectly manicured hand and ticked off, ''One man is dead, a car has been blown to smithereens, and your very own fiancé is missing. Don't you think we have some cause to be just the tiniest bit concerned about your well-being? Donelli would have a conniption if he knew you were thinking of staying in that house. You know he would.''

Amanda waved aside the observation. ''Joe has a conniption if I go out after dark. Besides, he's not around.''

"It's not as if he's gone off on vacation, Amanda. The man has vanished."

"You don't have to remind me of that," she snapped.

"Sorry, but maybe you needed reminding," Jenny Lee said obstinately. "You know I've always admired your tenacity, but maybe Oscar and Joe are right. There are times when you are entirely too reckless for your own good."

"She's right," Miss Martha concurred. "There are times, Amanda, when a little prudence is called for."

Amanda lost her fragile hold on her patience. "If you all are so damned worried, you can move in with me. Bring Larry along. Bring Oscar along. Maybe even a couple of hired bodyguards. No matter what you decide, though, I am going back there this afternoon."

Jenny Lee and Miss Martha exchanged helpless glances. "But why?" Jenny Lee said. "It'll only upset you."

"I'm upset now. At least if I'm there, I can tear that place apart room by room until I find something that will tell me what the hell happened to my fiancé."

She turned away before Jenny Lee and Miss Martha could see the tears shimmering on her lashes. She had finally allowed Jenny Lee and Larry to talk her into staying at Jenny Lee's, then had spent an endless night waiting for the phone to ring, praying for Joe to call and explain. She would even have been relieved to hear from a kidnapper. At least, then, she'd know exactly what they were up against. Instead, the night had been silent except for the sound of drunken neighbors splashing in the apartment complex pool and then later the persistent hum of crickets. She'd finally fallen asleep around dawn and Jenny Lee had let her sleep until after lunch time. The lack of sleep and all that wasted time when she should have been searching for Joe had left her edgy. She tried to blink back the tears, but Jenny Lee saw them.

He friend jumped up, looking contrite, and gave Amanda a quick, consoling hug. "I'm sorry. I didn't mean to make things worse. You know I didn't. Everything will be okay, sugar. Just let me pack a bag. You're not going back there alone."

"I will hire someone, then," Miss Martha said, her shoulders squared with new resolve. A disturbing gleam of excitement made her blue eyes sparkle.

"Hire someone?" Amanda said.

"A bodyguard."

"Oh, Lord," she groaned, regretting her earlier face-tious remark. "You don't need to do that," she said hurriedly.

"Yes, I do, if I'm to have a moment's peace. Now we'll not say another word about it." With that, she squeezed Amanda's hand and marched out. No general had set off to fulfill presidential orders with more determination. "I will be in touch, my dear."

Amanda watched her go with a sinking sensation in the pit of her stomach. Miss Martha seemed to have gotten hooked on Amanda's investigations. The next thing they knew, she'd be fancying herself as Miss Marple and meddling in everyone's lives. Amanda was going to have to come up with some way to discourage her before she got hurt.

In the meantime, though, she followed her outside so she could check her own car for evidence of tampering. At one time the action had been virtually a reflex, insisted on by the New York police who'd been assigned to protect her in the weeks following her revelations about corruption in the court system. With those men behind bars, she'd gotten careless since moving to Georgia. She'd been so sure that nothing could touch her here, an attitude fostered by her isolated existence and her mindless work for the *Gazette*. For all too long she hadn't reported on anything more provocative than quilting circle activities. Even her more recent investigative pieces for *Inside Atlanta* hadn't thrown her into the sort of danger she'd faced daily in New York as she'd worked to expose public officials who were using their offices for personal gain. Therefore, despite Jenny Lee's and Miss Martha's attack of nerves, she still couldn't believe that she herself was in any real danger.

Amanda was convinced, however, that Donelli had been the target of the bomber and, for the life of her, she couldn't imagine why, unless some crazed farmer had been jealous of the hearty size of his tomatoes. He was hardly leading a controversial lifestyle these days, unless you considered his attempt to grow Spanish onions in Vidalia country particularly daring.

There had to be something, though. Back at Joe's an hour later, with the hovering Jenny Lee consigned to making tea, she began her search. She started in the den again, even though she'd seen nothing especially odd on her cursory examination of his files the day before.

Though she hated the tedium, she resigned herself to a slow, methodical examination of each and every scrap of paper.

Jenny Lee returned with a pot of tea, two cups, and an assortment of Amanda's favorite jelly beans in a little crystal dish. "I thought you might like some," she said. "I couldn't find anything else in the kitchen anyway. I guess Joe cleaned out the refrigerator. I'll have to go out later and stock up."

"Whatever," Amanda said, taking one of the piña colada jelly beans and wishing herself onto that beach in Bermuda. It didn't work. The thought of her canceled honeymoon only made her sad. Which, in turn, made her angry and determined, so she supposed it had served a useful purpose.

"Come on, Jenny Lee. Help me sort this mess into some sort of order. Put anything that's obviously farm related over here. Personal correspondence can go next to it. Then make another stack of the miscellaneous stuff."

"What do you expect to find?"

"Beats me. The worst that can happen though is we'll get his files organized again."

As she'd expected, most of the papers were related to farm business. Apparently, he was operating in the black, though it appeared to be nip and tuck. Selling his own home-grown vegetables and his neighbor's peaches at one of those little roadside stands was hardly likely to turn much of a profit. To her ongoing frustration, he'd been perfectly content with his slow-paced, low-paying life. He'd enjoyed talking with the folks who stopped by, having lunch over at Virginia's bakery with men like Henry Lucas and Delbert Reed. Retreating from New York's violence, he had taken to the peaceful lifestyle at once, unlike Amanda who'd hated it from the first. It was only recently that she'd realized she was taking out on Georgia all the anger she had felt toward her ex-husband for abandoning her here.

"There are a whole bunch of personal letters here," Jenny Lee said. "Should I read them?"

"Who're they from?"

"One looks like it might be from his mother. Then there are these." She held up a whole batch. "Judging from the handwriting, I'd say they were from kids."

"Kids?" Amanda took the envelopes and studied the careful printing. She opened the first one and realized at once it was from a child Joe apparently sponsored through one of those foster parent plans. This particular boy lived in an impoverished section of Detroit. The others were from a little girl in Appalachia, a Navaho teenager, and half a dozen more scattered around the country, all excitedly reporting on school activities, sports, and their own troubled family lives.

"I wish you were here, Daddy Joe," one little boy wrote. "It's going to be father-son night at school soon and you could be my dad. I tell all my friends what a brave policeman you were and that someday you'll come to see me. Could you do that? I really need a dad, even if it's only make-believe. Your almost son, Todd."

Amanda's heart ached when she finished, partly for that little boy crying out for a father and partly for the man who'd tried in his own way to fill that role. It was a side of Joe she hadn't known existed. "I didn't know," she said to Jenny Lee, folding the letter carefully and tucking it back into its painstakingly addressed envelope. "He never said a word."

"Look here," Jenny Lee said. "There's a picture in this one."

The girl was tiny, her blonde hair shining clean and straight to her shoulders, her faded, too-big dress was perfectly pressed. Her winning, gap-toothed smile made Amanda want to smile back, but it was her eyes—big brown eyes that dominated her heart-shaped face—that touched the heart. Never before had Amanda seen such wistfulness and need. A feeling of total empathy sprang up for this child she'd never seen before.

"Are you okay?" Jenny Lee asked.

"Fine," she said briskly, defiantly ignoring the loneliness and fear. "Let me see the rest."

"The only one left is from a woman, another Donelli. Could be a sister or a cousin."

"Or his ex-wife," Amanda said and held out her hand for that, too. She hadn't realized he'd kept in touch with the woman who'd fallen for the glamour of his uniform, then walked out on him when the danger of police work had gotten to be too much for her.

It's just as well, he'd told Amanda, considering the move he'd eventually made to Georgia. *She'd have hated being so far from Bloomingdale's.*

Only now did she realize that the comment had been made with fond awareness, rather than rancor. No matter how often he'd told her he'd forgiven and forgotten, she hadn't believed him. She attributed her own fury at an ex-spouse to him, but this letter proved how wrong she'd been. Dated just the previous month, it was warmly affectionate. The strong bond between them obviously hadn't died with the divorce decree as it had between her and Mack.

She put the letter aside, then picked up the one from his mother. It was filled with regret over having to miss the sudden wedding, along with best wishes for their marriage and stern admonitions that he was to bring Amanda home to meet the family very soon. He'd read parts of it to her on Monday when it had arrived.

"I should call them, shouldn't I?" she said, hoping Jenny Lee would tell her no.

"Yes. If the police have already talked to them, they must be worried sick. Or Dave Michaels's wife could have said something. You said he and Donelli had known each other since they were kids. Their families probably know each other."

"I never even thought of that. I guess I kept hoping he'd turn up before we had to tell them anything. How can I call up and say, oh, by the way, I'm still not your daughter-in-law because your son seems to have disappeared."

"Maybe he's been in touch with them. Did you ever think of that?"

"If he could call anyone, it would be me."

"Not if he thought you might get dragged into the middle of things."

Amanda stared at her. Jenny Lee flushed. "Okay, forget that. He knows you'll be in the middle of things, no matter what he does to keep you out of it."

"So there wouldn't be any reason for him not to call, would there?"

"Unless he can't," Jenny Lee granted. "So, you'd better call his folks and tell them what's going on."

Amanda found Joe's address book, looked up the number, and set the phone on the floor in front of her. She couldn't seem to make herself dial. "I can't do it, Jenny Lee. I've interviewed families right after they get news like this. I know how devastating it can be. How can I do that to them?"

"Do you want them to hear it from somebody like that awful FBI guy?"

She imagined Jeffrey Dunne's cold, dispassionate delivery and picked up the receiver. A minute later, Mrs. Donelli was on the phone. Jenny Lee gave Amanda an encouraging pat, mouthed something about groceries, and left.

"Why, Amanda, what on earth are you doing calling here on your honeymoon?" Mrs. Donelli said. "Aren't you two in Bermuda?"

"I'm afraid not," she said, wishing she were at least there to deliver the bad news face to face. "Something happened yesterday."

She heard the sharply indrawn breath, then, "Oh, dear. Nothing serious. Not an accident. Joey didn't fall off that ridiculous tractor and hurt himself, did he?"

Amanda sensed an ally in her antifarming crusade and

stored the information away for later. "No. It's nothing like that. I don't want to alarm you, Mrs. Donelli, but Joe is missing. I was hoping maybe you'd heard from him?"

"Missing? You mean he disappeared after the wedding?"

"No, before."

"He stood you up?" she said incredulously. "Joey would never do that. We talked just last week. He sounded so happy. He couldn't wait for Saturday. He was so disappointed that we couldn't be there, but I explained again about his father's job and how he couldn't just up and take off at the last second to drive clear down there. He wanted us to fly. He even said he'd pay for the tickets. I know it's silly, but even for Joey's wedding I couldn't quite make myself get on one of those planes. Anyway, I just can't imagine him not showing up. Did you two have a fight?"

"No. Everything has been perfect. There's more, though." She told her what happened to Dave Michaels.

Mrs. Donelli gasped. "Oh, that dear boy! Oh, my, that's just terrible." Her composure faltered only for an instant, though, before she said briskly, "Now, Amanda, I want you to stay calm. As soon as I speak to Mr. Donelli, I'm going to take the next train right down there to be with you. I should have done that in the first place. If I'd been there . . ."

"Please, don't think that. You couldn't have stopped this."

"Well, I'm coming now, just the same."

The thought of Mrs. Donelli's warm Italian mothering

held a certain appeal, but Amanda knew it would be a terrible mistake to let her come. She wasn't sure she could bear to see her own worry reflected in Mrs. Donelli's eyes. It was bad enough that Jenny Lee and Miss Martha were hovering over her. "No, please. There's no need for you to do that. I promise to let you know the minute I find out anything. Stay there. If he's in trouble and can't call here, Joe may try to reach you."

There was a long hesitation before Mrs. Donelli finally said, "I suppose that's possible, but what about you? Are you all alone down there?"

"I have a friend staying at the house with me. I'll be fine. Please don't worry, Mrs. Donelli. I'm going to find him."

"Joey's told me what a fine reporter you are, Amanda, so I'm sure you will. You call me, though, if there is anything we can do here. I won't get a minute's rest until I know he's safe."

"Neither will I, Mrs. Donelli. Neither will I."

She hung up, then glanced up to see Detective Harrison lurking in the doorway, his graying hair windblown, his tan suit mussed, his tie askew and dotted with either ketchup or a very modern design. It looked as though he'd had another long night, bolstered by fast food and caffeine.

"I knocked," he apologized. "I guess you didn't hear me. I saw the car outside, so I knew you were here."

"I was on the phone."

"You shouldn't be here all by yourself."

She scowled at him. "Don't you start on me, too. Besides, Jenny Lee's just gone to the store."

He nodded toward the stacks of paper. "Find anything?"

She shook her head.

"Have you come up with any theories?"

She stared at him, surprised. "You're asking me?"

His expression turned rueful. "I never once said you didn't have a good head on your shoulders, Amanda. You just have this disturbing tendency to circumvent procedures."

It was a familiar complaint. Joe had voiced it with regularity. "Police procedures," she retorted. "By journalistic standards, I'm just doing my job."

"You have a vested interest in this one, though, don't you? Isn't there some rule about conflict of interest?"

"Who says I'm going to report on this particular story?"

"In which case we come back to circumventing the law."

She grinned at the tidy trap he'd set for her. "An interesting quandary."

"Fascinating," he agreed.

"Don't try to talk me into staying out of this."

He sighed. "Believe me, I wouldn't waste my breath. Of course, maybe, just this once, we could work a deal."

She sat up a little straighter and studied his expression as he settled on the edge of the sofa. He looked perfectly serious. "A deal? You mean like a partnership?"

A faint smile teased at his mouth. "I thought that might get your attention."

"I don't usually work with the cops."

"So I've noticed," he said dryly. "Could you make an exception, just this once, seeing as how you're not working a story? I saw how you bristled yesterday when Jeffrey Dunne said you were on the same side, but maybe you and I could cooperate."

She considered her options. At the moment, this was far and away the best. Jim Harrison had access to information she might find difficult to get. Though she didn't understand his motivation, from the sound of it, he might even be inclined to bend a few rules in her favor. "Unofficially, right?"

"Unofficially. We share information. You don't go chasing down leads without my knowing about it."

"And vice versa?"

This time he actually chuckled. "Okay. And vice versa."

"Why are you doing this?"

"I have my reasons."

"You just want to be sure you know what I'm up to."

"That's one reason," he admitted. "I figure I owe that to Donelli. I know how he liked to dog your footsteps to keep you out of mischief."

"And?"

"And just once I'd like to prove to Jeffrey Dunne exactly what an ass he is."

"Sounds like you've run into the FBI agent before."

"On several occasions. He's an arrogant, pompous bureaucrat."

"Come on, Detective Harrison. Don't be so diplomatic,'' she teased, surprised by the slip in his natural discretion. "What do you really think of the man?"

He turned the tables on her with an alacrity she'd come to admire. "What did you think of him?"

She considered the question thoughtfully. "Arrogant about sums it up. I also got the distinct impression he doesn't play fair."

"Meaning?"

"As long as we're sharing information, I noticed something very odd about his thorough search of the premises. Remember all that talk about tampering with evidence?"

"Yeah. What about it?"

"Well, I can't lay this squarely on him, but somebody cleaned out the guest room."

"Meaning?"

"I know Dave Michaels only flew down for the wedding, but it seems to me that he had to have more with him than the tuxedo on his back. There was no evidence in that guest room to indicate he'd ever been here."

"Maybe he was staying in a hotel."

"No way. Joe and I picked him up at the airport and brought him straight here. Joe carried his bag upstairs himself."

"So, what do you make of that?"

"Well, I don't think the bomber bothered to pack Dave's things. That leaves the FBI."

"But why?" he said, almost to himself.

"Evidence?" she speculated.

"Maybe, but I have a gut-level hunch it was more than that. So do you apparently." He met Amanda's gaze, his expression was thoughtful. "Let's go take another look at that room."

The small guest room was tucked under the eaves. Its slanted ceiling was not the best for guests as tall as Dave Michaels or Jim Harrison. Harrison had to stoop as he circled the room. She watched in fascination as he moved about idly. Then she caught the alertness in his eyes and realized that he was taking in every detail. She tried to view the room through his eyes.

The quirky ceiling gave it a certain coziness, reminding her of some Louisa May Alcott setting. She had played to that old-fashioned, storybook feeling with her choice of a blue and beige wallpaper with its tiny sprigs of flowers and the priscilla curtains that billowed now in the breeze. The double bed was an antique four-poster. The only other furniture in the room was the matching tall mahogany chest opposite the foot of the bed. There wasn't so much as a dust swirl to investigate as far as she could see.

"I told you," she said. "There's not a trace. I doubt if they've even left a fingerprint behind."

"What's in the dresser?"

"Some extra blankets. That's it."

"Have you looked?"

"No."

He grinned at her. "You're slipping, Amanda. Maybe the man was a neatness freak. Maybe he put his clothes in the drawers and his suitcase in the closet."

"Maybe," she said doubtfully, but she began opening drawers anyway. Detective Harrison began tearing the bed apart, then moved on to the closet as Amanda reached the last drawer. As she'd expected, there were two blankets in it.

"Nothing," she said. "What about you?"

"Not a thing," he admitted, clearly disappointed.

She started closing the drawers. The bottom one stuck. She stuck her hand in to press the blankets down, but the drawer was still jammed.

"What's wrong?"

"I can't get it to close."

"Pull it all the way out." He bent down to help her. When the drawer was out, he put his hand inside the dresser, reaching all the way to the back.

Amanda caught the beginning of a triumphant smile even before she saw the file folder. It was a plain, unlabeled folder and very thin. Still, she felt a familiar stirring of excitement. "What is it?"

She leaned over his shoulder as he flipped it open. Inside were no more than half a dozen newspaper clippings, all dated two or more years before, all about Federal Judge Bryan Price.

"Why would a file on Judge Price be stuck in the dresser?" Amanda wondered. "Isn't he the one who was killed with that mail bomb?"

As the implications of her words sank in, Amanda's gaze shot to Detective Harrison. "Oh, my God."

He nodded. "My sentiments exactly. I don't know what your friend was doing with these clippings, but one thing's for sure, it puts his death in a whole new light."

"Maybe," Amanda said slowly.

He regarded her curiously. "What are you thinking?"

"Couldn't the clippings have belonged to Joe?"

"But why would he have stuck them in here? Why not in the desk downstairs?"

"Safekeeping?"

"It's just a file of old clippings, Amanda."

"Maybe so, but my guess is that directly or indirectly Dave Michaels got killed because of something in that file. All we have to do is figure out what."

C H A P T E R

Five

*E*VERYONE—well, obviously not *everyone*—had liked and respected fifty-one-year-old U.S. District Court Judge Bryan Price. The Fourth of July mail bomb that had killed him in 1989 had sent shock waves through Georgia. Amanda and Mack had moved south in the midst of the furor. She would have given anything to have worked on that story, but when she'd finally been hired by Oscar as a reporter for his rural weekly newspaper, he'd had other things in mind for her. Boring things. Stories with the substance of cotton candy. Features about as controversial as milk. It had almost driven her crazy, especially with a story as complicated as the Price murder just waiting for her brand of investigative journalism.

Oscar, however, had not been remotely impressed by Amanda's New York credentials. He ran a small local paper with few aspirations beyond reporting the high school football scores accurately. As he had enjoyed reminding her, he'd hired someone to cover community activities and that did not include a murder way over in Atlanta. Now that he was editor of *Inside Atlanta* he was a little more open-minded and daring about her assignments. She still wrote occasional fluff, but he also allowed her to tackle the kind of hard-hitting investigative pieces she'd been honored for up north. With a little nudging and a few dangled promises of national journalistic recognition, perhaps now he would let her start digging into the Bryan Price murder for her next assignment. It was a fine line, but that wouldn't be exactly like reporting on Joe's disappearance.

"How much do you know about Bryan Price?" she asked Jim Harrison, adding, "Things these clippings won't tell me."

"I met him once or twice. He was an incredible man, totally dedicated to the law, yet absolutely devoted to his wife and kids. He also had an amazing knack for remembering names and faces. The second time I ran into him, he not only recognized me, but asked about my golf game. It was still every bit as lousy as the first time we'd discussed it. We commiserated over the frustration of whacking a little white ball several hundred yards into a hole the size of a measuring cup, when a sizable water hazard was so much easier to hit." He smiled at the memory, the first genuine smile Amanda could ever recall seeing on the detective's normally taciturn face.

"You liked him."

"Liked and admired. He really was a great guy."

"No enemies?"

"No more than any other judge who hears controversial cases and none that were personal as far as I knew. There was never the slightest suggestion that anyone from his private life was under suspicion."

"What about the sort of decisions he handed down? Liberal? Conservative?"

"Fair."

"Political ambitions? Was he aiming for the Supreme Court?"

"I'm sure that's every federal judge's dream, but I wouldn't describe him as a political creature."

"Did you work on the murder investigation?"

His expression hardened again. "Briefly," he said tersely.

The reply and tone surprised her. "How come? He was killed in Atlanta, wasn't he?"

"Yes. At home in Buckhead. The bomb arrived with the Saturday mail. Our forensics people never really got much of a look at it."

Again, there was that unmistakable bitter edge to his voice, that glint of barely concealed anger in his eyes. Comprehension finally dawned on her. "Jeffrey Dunne?"

"Precisely. His turf. Everything went to the FBI lab. I suppose I would have been irritated no matter what the case had been, but the fact that the victim was a man I admired really galled the hell out of me. I wanted that killer."

"How did Dunne handle the investigation?"

"They never made an arrest. Personally, I thought he was too quick to jump on the obvious."

"Meaning?"

"Price was hearing a big drug case at the time. According to all the published reports, Dunne decided that was the link to the killing. When he couldn't come up with enough to make an arrest, he let it go, slapped it in some cold case file and forgot about it."

"Maybe he checked out other leads and they didn't pan out."

"Or maybe he's just a lousy investigator. There's no point in rehashing what happened in the past. Let's start from where we are now. Those clippings either belonged to Joe or Dave Michaels. Let's say they were Joe's. Why would he have them?"

Amanda could imagine only one reason. "Someone had hired him to continue the investigation."

Harrison nodded. "That makes the most sense to me. I'll make some calls, starting with Price's wife to see if anyone in the family contacted him. Now what about Dave? Can you think of any reason why he would have it? What do you know about him?"

"Not much," she admitted. "I only spent an hour or two with him last night before he and Joe took off for the bachelor party. It was the first time we'd met."

"Did you form an impression?"

She thought about the question. "Not really. He seemed a little distant, a little uptight, except when he and Joe were reminiscing. Then he came alive and I could see why they'd been such close friends. They have . . . *had* the same sense of humor, the same offbeat perspective. He and Joe grew up together in Brooklyn and they had a lot of stories to tell. They were on the same football teams, played pickup basketball games, double-dated, that kind of thing.''

''College?''

''I think that's when they headed their separate ways. Dave went away to some Ivy League school. Donelli worked, took some courses, then applied to become a cop.''

''But they stayed in touch?''

''Always.''

''What does he do for a living?''

Amanda started to say something, then stopped, amazed. ''I don't really know.''

''For a minute there, it looked as though you did.''

''I guess it was just an impression I had, that he was a scientist or a doctor or something. I seem to recall Joe mentioning a lab. It's not as if we ever sat down and discussed all his old friends. He'd mention names from time to time, incidents, but Joe's very much a man who lives in the present. He is much more likely to talk about the guys he had lunch with or what the mayor is likely to do about the potholes on Main Street.''

''Can you find out something more about Dave?''

''I'll call Mrs. Donelli back. She must know.''

''Why not call his wife? It would be natural enough under the circumstances. Her guard will be down. You could learn a lot more.''

Amanda nodded reluctantly. Unlike her go-for-the-

jugular style with the politically or morally corrupt, she
was a marshmallow when it came to something like this.
She hated preying on vulnerable sources. She avoided it
whenever possible. Unfortunately, this time she could
hardly escape it. They needed information Dave Michaels's
wife might be able to provide. She glanced at her watch
and was relieved to discover that it was almost time for
Delbert Reed's town meeting. She could at least put the
call off until later. She justified the delay as a way to give
Dave's wife a little longer with her private grief. Marshmallow reasoning.

"I'll call tonight as soon as I get back from the town
meeting," she promised. "Are you coming?"

He grimaced. "No. I think I'll pass on that. You keep
me posted."

After Jim Harrison left, Amanda's confidence rose for
the first time since the bombing. She felt as if she were
back in control, her thoughts focused, the first real thread
in hand. Joe was out there somewhere and she was going
to find him. Tonight's town meeting, filled with prospective witnesses and maybe even a suspect or two, would
be another step in that direction. She called the sheriff's
office to see where it was being held.

"The First Baptist Church," Buford reported.

Somebody, it seemed, had a wicked sense of humor.
The last place Amanda wanted to spend the evening was
the church where her wedding was to have taken place.

She went anyway, Jenny Lee grumbling all the way
that she shouldn't be putting herself through such an
ordeal.

"And what should I be doing? Languishing at home, waiting for the kidnapper to call? Besides, I want to see Delbert Reed in action. I hear the mayor has quite a flair for the dramatic."

Jenny Lee wrinkled her nose. "He got elected, didn't he? I think the only reason he did was because everyone recognized him from those late-night commercials for his car dealership. If he could sell those old clunkers, he could sell anything."

"He's in his second term, though. He can't be that bad."

"I suppose not, but I can't think of a single thing he's actually done, unless you count the fact that there are four parking meters in front of the hardware store. He says that's the town's road fund."

Amanda groaned. "No wonder those potholes keep getting deeper."

As they approached the front of the church, Miss Martha and the ladies from her historic preservation group formed a clucking, sympathetic circle around Amanda. As far as she could tell, none of these frail ladies were meant to be her bodyguard. Amanda wondered if Miss Martha had actually followed through on her vow to hire protection.

"I don't know what Delbert was thinking of having this meeting here," Miss Martha declared, bristling with indignation on Amanda's behalf.

"It's as good as anyplace," Amanda said with a shrug.

"Oh, you are so brave," Henrietta Cosgrove told her. "Isn't she brave, girls?"

"Oh, yes," Eleanor Mae Taylor agreed.

"Oh my, yes," chorused the rest, all of whom shared Miss Martha's maternal fondness for Amanda. They'd also elevated her to the status of heroine for finding the culprit who'd been involved in trying to cheat them out of their sanity and their most prized possessions.

"Let's get inside and take a seat right down front so we can all hear," Miss Martha said, ushering them inside. There was no argument. Even Amanda knew better than to counter Miss Martha's wishes when she was reigning over her ladies. Besides, for all of her brave front, she wasn't looking forward to walking alone down that aisle. She was glad of the supportive company.

The front of the chapel was still decorated with the huge displays of peach roses and white orchids that had been meant for her ceremony. Heads turned as she made her way to the front pew; voices dropped to whispers. Miss Martha cast a stern glare at the gossipers until they fell silent.

As soon as she had taken her seat, Amanda looked around for Oscar. As the owner and editor of the weekly *Gazette*, he'd been considered a mover and shaker around town. When he'd moved on to *Inside Atlanta*, his influential role in town politics hadn't ceased. He was consulted on everything from development to the county fair. Besides all that and even after the rocky beginning of their journalistic relationship, Amanda considered him one of the closest friends she and Joe had. But she didn't see him anywhere. It was downright peculiar that he wouldn't show up for the meeting. Nor, come to think of it, had he called since early that morning when Jenny Lee had apparently talked to him. For a man who almost always had one ear glued to a phone, his failure to return her call in itself was odd.

Before she could ask Jenny Lee if anyone else had talked to Oscar, Delbert Reed came forward and began addressing the crowd from the pulpit. His complexion was ruddy, his sandy hair slicked back from a handsome face that showed faint signs of alcoholic puffiness. In another few years, if he wasn't careful, he'd lose his looks and take on an unhealthy paunchiness. That probably wouldn't diminish his smooth charm, which radiated through the chapel like so much air freshener, sweet scented and thoroughly false. His voice rose to the occasion like a man used to reading from the Gospel.

"You all know why we've gathered here tonight and I'd like the Reverend Hawkins to get things off to the right start by leading us in a little prayer."

So much for separation of church and state, Amanda thought.

Seth, looking uncomfortable at having his place at the pulpit usurped in his own church, approached the microphone. It clanged and screeched as he lowered it for his own considerably shorter height. Then in a tone filled with Sunday morning resonance even more powerful than the mayor's, he prayed for Dave Michaels's eternal soul. He prayed for Joe. He prayed for the success of the search for the killer. And, just for good measure, he prayed for everyone in the room, who'd shown such love and community concern by showing up tonight.

"And especially for our own Sheriff Eldon Mason, who faces the daunting task of solving this terrible crime."

That, Amanda thought, would come as a surprise to Jeffrey Dunne, who as an outsider apparently wasn't worthy of Seth's prayers.

As soon as the preacher had stepped out of the way and before Delbert could get back to the mike, Jeeter Potts, who owned the combination laundromat and newsstand in town, stood up and hitched his jeans up over his ample belly. He demanded to know what was being done to protect innocent citizens from this obviously crazed bomber.

"My wife's afraid to go out after dark. She's home right this minute with the drapes drawn and the TV on for company. She's got a shotgun resting on her knees."

Amanda nearly groaned aloud. According to local gossip, Francie Potts spent every night in front of the television with her shotgun in her lap. She swore she hadn't felt safe since someone stole the Spiegel catalogue out of her mailbox ten years before. "Right out of the box," she liked to tell anyone who asked. "And it was nigh on Christmastime, too. Had to do every bit of my shopping over in Atlanta." The latter was declared as if she'd been asked to shop in hell itself.

"Now, Jeeter, I don't think there's any need for Francie to be overwrought," Delbert said smoothly. "Ain't that right, Eldon?"

Eldon stood up. His voice boomed from the choir loft without benefit of the microphone. "Yes, sir. This here's one of those random things, as best we can tell so far. Why, the man who was killed wasn't even from around here. I figure some big city guy like that probably had a whole lot of enemies we couldn't possibly even know about. Otherwise, why would the Federal Bureau of Investigation be involved?''

The mention of the FBI drew startled mutterings all around the room. Even Miss Martha appeared stunned. "Amanda, dear, what do you know about this?"

"Not much," she admitted. "They were there, but they haven't explained their presence to me."

"Then you must ask. I'm surprised at you."

Amanda stared at her and nodded slowly. She really must have been rattled last night. The most obvious question hadn't even occurred to her. She'd been so busy trying to get inside the house, she'd never really demanded to know why the FBI had claimed jurisdiction in the case and done it so swiftly, too. "You're absolutely right, Miss Martha," she said with renewed resolve.

Miss Martha patted her hand. "It's natural that you wouldn't be thinking clearly, my dear. After all, this has been a terrible blow, but we can't let that drag us down now, can we?"

"No," Amanda said obediently, then with more conviction, "no, we can't."

While Miss Martha was chiding her, Henry Lucas expressed his dismay at the impression this was likely to have on prospective businesses. Henry took great pride in his role at the helm of the chamber of commerce. As a realtor, it was in his best interest to see that the town grew and prospered. Everyone said this had been a modern version of a one-horse town till Henry had gotten everyone organized and working together. Few dared to mention that with the borders of Atlanta practically splitting at the seams, the spillover quite naturally was heading in this direction. No matter whose doing it was in reality, Henry was clearly dismayed by the prospect of losing even an inch of the ground he'd worked so hard to gain.

"We can't let a reputation as a center of crime get out to the world, if we expect more development in these parts," he declared.

"Who needs more development?" demanded Henrietta, leaping to her feet beside Amanda. Henrietta was tall and reed-thin and when she drew herself up in indignation, she was an impressive sight. "If you ask me, development is the cause of things like this. This was a peaceful little area until they started putting in all those fast-food places and strip malls." She sat back down, glaring pointedly at Henry all the while.

Three others were on their feet to agree before Delbert shouted them down. "We are getting mighty far afield here now. We are here to determine what we can do to help Eldon find the criminal behind this murder."

"We can't do a damn thing," Jeeter said. "Eldon's got all that fancy new equipment and access to those computerized fingerprint things in Atlanta. Let him and Buford do the job they were paid to do. What the devil do we pay taxes for, if not for that?"

Miss Martha's cheeks turned an indignant pink. She

pounded her cane against the floor until she had absolute quiet. She glared across the aisle. "Jeeter Potts, you always were a self-centered fool. What happens to one in this community can just as well happen to all of us. Therefore, it behooves us to stick together. I think we should form a citizens' crime commission right here and now."

A chorus of murmurs indicated strong agreement for the notion. Apparently, only Amanda noted that most of those murmurs were coming from the front pew right next to Miss Martha.

"Good idea," Delbert said, seizing the momentum. "I'd like to appoint George Tolliver as its head."

Amanda leaned over to ask Miss Martha, "Who's he?"

Miss Martha shot a look of disgust at the mayor. "One of Delbert's toadies. Hasn't worked a lick in the last ten years, as near as I can tell. Made some money in insurance. Sold roofing for awhile. He has the slickest tongue this side of a courtroom, but not much brain to back it up."

"Can he actually lead an investigation?"

"Of course not, but it'll keep 'em all out of your hair while you do what needs to be done."

A slow grin spread across Amanda's face. "Why, you really are a sneaky devil, Miss Martha," she said admiringly.

"You don't live around a place like this your whole life without learning how to get things done," she replied. She sat back, looking smug.

A moment later, Delbert called the meeting to a close and invited everyone to stop by the rectory for punch and cookies. Amanda had every intention of missing that, but Delbert had other ideas.

"You must come along," he insisted. "George will need your input on this commission thing."

"I really don't think so."

"Go on," Miss Martha said with a definite twinkle in her eyes. "I think you'll find it illuminating."

Horrifying was the term Amanda would have used. Even though Delbert introduced her to George Tolliver, the man never had an opportunity to say a word. Either Delbert or Henry Lucas was always close by to put words—thoroughly innocuous words at that—right into his mouth. Amanda finally sent them after more punch. As soon as they were gone, Tolliver said, "Have . . . have you heard anything about Joe? Nice man. Had some of his tomatoes just the other night. The wife canned them last summer," he noted proudly.

"There's still no word."

"Don't suppose . . . don't suppose he just, uh, you know. Could he have just decided . . ."

"Not to get married?"

He blinked rapidly and embarrassment turned his cheeks bright red. "Yes. Sorry, don't mean to insult you. Man would have to be a fool to walk away from a pretty little thing like you."

"I'm not insulted. Joe did not stand me up, Mr. Tolliver. I think the car bombing and the death of his friend are quite enough to explain his failure to show at the church.''

"Kidnappers. Should have ... I would think they'd have asked for ... ransom.''

"Maybe that's not what this is about," Amanda said. "They may not be after money.''

"What then?''

"When I figure that out, Mr. Tolliver, I'll let you know.''

Dismay spread across his round face. "But that's my job," he protested.

She smiled agreeably. "Then I'm sure you'll let me know the minute you've figured it out.''

Chances were, hell would freeze over first.

Before Amanda could make her escape, the man who owned the property next to Joe's approached her, smiling shyly. Harley Griggs was twisting his straw hat in his huge, roughened hands. "Ms. Roberts.''

"Amanda," she corrected.

He nodded. "Yes, ma'am. Just wanted you to know if there's anything I can do to help out 'til Joe gets back, you just have to ask. Don't imagine you know too much about farming and such.''

"Not a thing, as a matter of fact.''

"Then if it's okay with you, I'll just stop by now and again and look things over, do whatever needs doing.''

"Harley, that would be wonderful," she said gratefully. "I really would appreciate it and I know Joe would, too.''

"Just being neighborly. Joe helped me out last summer, when my tractor broke. Figure I owe him." He started away, then came back. "You know, I been puzzling about something tonight. Nobody said much about Joe being missing and all, since everybody's so het up about that murder. You heard from him?"

Amanda shook her head.

"I expect you will real soon, then. When he took off the other day, he looked to be in a real hurry. He probably didn't have a chance to call you."

"What?" Amanda said, grabbing his forearm so hard he winced. "Sorry. You saw Joe leave?"

"I surely did. Must have been ten, maybe fifteen minutes after that bomb blast. Took off across the back, him and another man."

"Did it look like the other man had a gun? Was he forcing Joe to leave?"

"Not so's I could tell. Then, again, I don't see so good without my specs on."

Amanda tried to hide her disappointment. "I don't suppose you got a good look at the other man, then, either?"

"Can't say as I did. I recognized Joe from his size and all, but the other one didn't look at all familiar."

She tried to drag details from his memory anyway. Witnesses often saw far more than they realized. "Was he the same height as Joe? Shorter? Taller? What about his coloring?"

He twisted his hat, looking increasingly miserable. "Sorry. I guess I was still too discombobulated from that bomb going off to pay much attention. At the time I thought they was just getting out of the way in case of another explosion.''

''Was this before or after the police arrived?''

''Let me think a minute. As I recall, they was just pulling in.''

''Have you told anyone else about this?''

''No, ma'am. Nobody's asked. Guess they figured I was at the church, like everybody else, but the missus got sick, so I stayed home to watch over her. Does that help some?''

''Yes, Harley. It helps a lot.''

It told her for one thing that Joe had been alive yesterday afternoon after the bombing. Unfortunately, it didn't give her a clue about where he was now or who had been with him when he'd taken off.

C H A P T E R

Six

AMANDA was already on her third cup of caffeine-loaded coffee and her fourth walk through the house by the time Jenny Lee stumbled into the kitchen on Monday morning, wearing Larry's Atlanta Braves T-shirt. With her thoughts churning every which way and impatient to begin making some sort of progress in the search for Donelli, Amanda hadn't slept a wink. All that futile introspection had made her exceedingly grumpy.

"Do you have any idea what kind of fool I am?" she demanded, blocking Jenny Lee's path to the counter.

Jenny Lee yawned. "Can I have some of that coffee if I guess right?"

"I'm serious."

"So am I."

Amanda regarded Jenny Lee with fascination. "You

aren't so perky in the mornings, are you?'' she said, her own mood improving tremendously at the discovery.

"No. I put it on with my makeup.''

"Larry must love that.''

"Larry doesn't know it.''

"Oh?''

"He sleeps later than I do.''

"I see.''

Jenny Lee closed her eyes as she sipped the strong coffee. She sighed blissfully. "Better,'' she said finally. "Now what was it you were saying about being a fool?''

"I should have told Joe how I felt about him.''

"He knew, Amanda.''

"But I should have said it, instead of saving it all up for the ceremony. I spend my whole life hunting for the perfect word to describe a person or express an emotion, but when it came to telling Joe I loved him, I clammed up.''

"Well, I guess you'll just have to find him and tell him now.''

"Maybe I'll never have that chance.''

Jenny Lee cut her off sternly. "Now, you stop that right this minute, Amanda Roberts. Joe is just fine and you are going to find him. I won't have you thinking any other way.''

"I can't help it. Why hasn't he called? Why hasn't a kidnapper called? What the hell is going on?''

"You said last night that Harley Griggs saw him leaving here after the bombing with somebody. Kidnappers aren't like the cops. They don't generally allow you one call to your lawyer or your fiancée. Maybe you'll get a call today. If you'd stay put, he'd have a better chance of reaching you. You've been running all over hell and gone, since the minute this started.''

"I was at your place all day yesterday."

"All morning yesterday," Jenny Lee corrected. "You were here yesterday afternoon and at the meeting last night."

"Okay, okay. But I can't just stay put. I can't conduct an investigation from the living room."

"You do it from the office all the time. That's what phones are for. Just think of all the hotels and motels you could call. Maybe the kidnapper's holed up in one of them."

"I doubt if they've booked into a Holiday Inn."

"Then try all those little places along the back roads, the ones with the cute little cabins and kitchenettes and the sign outside that flashes Vacancy, usually with one of the letters missing. They've got phones. They've probably even got lonely, talkative managers."

"Now you sound like Oscar. Speaking of whom, do you have any idea where he was last night?"

"Not a clue. It was downright peculiar that he wasn't at the meeting, wasn't it? I know he knew about it, because he mentioned it when he called in the morning. I guess he just got tied up at work."

"It was Sunday. Oscar does not drive all the way into Atlanta on Sunday."

"So, maybe his wife fried chicken and he couldn't bear to miss it. He's been talking about the way her

Sunday dinners used to be ever since he started this diet. Fried chicken and mashed potatoes and gravy would definitely keep him home.''

Amanda stared at her. ''The way your mind works frightens me.''

Jenny Lee smiled contentedly. ''That's what Joe's always saying about you.''

''I don't think he means it as a compliment,'' Amanda said with a sigh. ''Get dressed, Jenny Lee. I want to get to the office.''

Jenny Lee looked aghast. ''You can't do that. Didn't you hear a word I said?''

''All of them.''

''Well, then, what if the kidnapper calls?''

''I'm sure if he wants me, he'll find me at the office.''

''But it wouldn't look right.''

''Do you think I care about that? I really need to start tackling this mess and my mind works best in an office environment. Besides, if I'm going to work the phones like you said, I need my numbers. They're all on the Rolodex at work.''

''Haven't you ever heard of the Yellow Pages?''

''They're not nearly as complete as my Rolodex. Now, are you coming or not?''

''I'm coming.''

Jenny Lee grumbled all the way into Atlanta. Amanda felt like strangling her. Then she saw the stunned expression on Oscar's face and decided maybe she was the one who was out of step. Maybe she should be languishing around with an attack of the vapors, after all, but it wasn't her style. She was driven under the best of conditions, but her motivation to uncover the truth now was stronger than ever before.

"Not you, too," she warned Oscar as she stomped past him.

"I didn't say a word," he said, trailing after her. "Did you hear me say a word?"

"Keep it that way."

"Why are you here?"

"Oscar, I warned you."

"I can't help it. It's a natural question."

"I have calls to make. I work better here. Is that good enough?"

"What calls?"

"For starters I want to check out all those little out-of-the-way motels to see if they've stashed Joe someplace like that. Then I need to reach Dave Michaels's wife. We found some clippings hidden in the guest room and I need to know for sure if they're linked to him."

"What kind of clippings?"

"About Judge Price's murder."

He regarded her blankly. "Why the devil would Dave have those?"

"That's what I want to find out. By the way, where were you last night?"

He ran his fingers through the remaining hairs on his head and avoided her gaze. "I got tied up with something."

"About the bombing?"

"No."

Amanda glanced at him sharply, but his expression was closed.

"You want some coffee?" he asked, ending the discussion.

Amanda relented more quickly than usual. She supposed Oscar was entitled to his secrets the same as the rest of them. "No more coffee," she said with a shudder. "If I have any more caffeine, I'm likely to use a letter opener to go after the next person who bugs me."

Oscar nodded. "I'll be in my office."

"I'll be at my desk," Jenny Lee added.

Amanda smiled at them wearily as they discreetly backed away. "It's swell to know we're all accounted for." She turned to her desk and put them both out of her mind. She pulled Joe's address book from her purse. The first thing would be to call Dave Michaels's wife. She flipped through the pages, but there was no phone number or address, not under Michaels, not even under the *D*'s for Dave. How odd! She knew this was the only place Donelli kept phone numbers. Unlike her, he never scribbled them inside the phone directory or jotted them on scraps of paper.

So, she would have to call Mrs. Donelli back, after all. As soon as she had her on the line, she brought her up to date on the scanty developments, then explained what she needed.

"Dear, I'm sorry. I don't have his number, not since he left home years ago."

"What about his parents, then? I suppose I could call them."

"They moved a few years back. Someplace in Arizona, I think."

"Never mind, then. I can probably get Dave's number from information. Do you have any idea what street he lived on?"

"Street? I'm not even sure what city he lived in."

"But I thought he lived in New York."

"No. He hasn't lived up here for at least five years, maybe longer. I'm very certain of that, dear."

Amanda fell silent. This made no sense at all. She could have sworn that Donelli had said Dave was flying down from New York. She tried to recall their exact conversation, but she had been so wrapped up in wedding preparations, nothing else had really registered.

But dammit, she just knew Joe had said Dave was in New York. *He'll be catching a flight from LaGuardia.* Yes. That was what he'd said. The exact words.

"Amanda," Mrs. Donelli said. "Are you okay?"

"I'm fine. I'm just a little confused. Why would Joe have lied about something like that?"

"Are you certain he did, dear?"

"Yes. I remember exactly what he told me now. He said Dave was taking a flight out of LaGuardia."

"Could Dave have been in New York on business, then?"

Amanda sighed. "I suppose that's possible," she conceded. "If any of the neighbors up there happen to know where to find Dave's wife or his family, let me know, will you? Maybe there will be some sort of obituary in the paper.''

"This is important, isn't it?"

"It could be. I just don't know anymore."

"Then I'll call at once, if I can locate any information. You be careful, Amanda. Stay safe until Joey gets back."

"I will, Mrs. Donelli. I'll do my very best."

When she'd hung up, she stared out the windows at the Atlanta skyline. What now? She couldn't very well start calling every information operator in Arizona and try to track down Dave's parents. If it came to that, though, she would do it. Maybe Mrs. Donelli would come through with a clue from one of her neighbors. In the meantime, she could start calling around to area motels. It was a long shot, but she was willing to try anything.

Two hours and three dozen unproductive calls later, Amanda gave up. If somebody was holding Donelli anywhere between Atlanta and Athens, they weren't hiding him in a motel room. She determinedly blanked out images of him being tied up in some shed, suffering from the continuing heat wave. Maybe when she got home tonight, she'd go out and interview some of the other adjoining property owners to see if any of them had seen Donelli being taken away on the day of the bombing. Maybe one of them had glimpsed an unfamiliar car or pickup truck in the area.

In the meantime, she was going to arrange to see Jeffrey Dunne and ask him the questions she should have asked on Saturday night.

Unfortunately, trying to get an appointment with Dunne

turned out to be more difficult than trying to breach White House security. Amanda lost patience with the process sometime after noon.

"I'm out of here," she announced as she headed for the elevator.

"Where?" Jenny Lee and Oscar inquired in a chorus.

"The FBI."

"Amanda, I wouldn't do that if I were you," Oscar said.

"Why not? I have questions. They, presumably, have answers."

"You don't think they're going to share them with a reporter, do you?"

"No, but they'd better damn sight share them with one of the victims or I'll raise a fuss they'll hear clear up on Capitol Hill."

"I'm sure they'll be terrified," Oscar retorted.

Her bravado diminished a little. "I have to try."

He nodded. "Okay. I know you do. Just don't go flashing your *Inside Atlanta* ID at them. This is personal."

"You don't think there's a story here?"

"I didn't say that. I just said you won't be the one doing it."

"And what about Judge Price's murder? How about letting me look into that?"

"That case is old news, Amanda. We're not doing historical perspective pieces. This is *Inside Atlanta* we're running here. It implies a certain timeliness."

"If I link the judge's death to Dave's murder will that make it timely enough for you?"

Oscar struggled with his obvious desire for a journalistic coup versus his scruples about conflict of interest. "Just watch your step. Things start hitting too close to home, you ask for help. There's no need to jeopardize the power of a piece like that with the notion that you've got some personal axe to grind. Is that clear?"

"As a bell. May I go now?"

"Go. Do what you have to do. Investigate. Be careful."

"And don't forget to come back for me," Jenny Lee said, watching Amanda's departure with apparent envy.

Getting away from Oscar and Jenny Lee turned out to be a piece of cake compared to tracking down Jeffrey Dunne. For a few minutes she wasn't sure the receptionist was even going to admit he existed. When she finally, grudgingly, did concede that much, she declined to add where he might be found.

"He's working on a case," she said with something that almost resembled parental pride.

"I know," Amanda said patiently. "I am part of that case."

"Are you a witness?"

"Not exactly."

"Are you related to the victim?"

"Victims," Amanda corrected. "There were two."

"I only know of one."

"Trust me. One man died. Another one is missing."

"Really," she said skeptically. "And are you related to either of them."

"Not exactly."

"Well, then, I don't see how I can help you."

"The kidnapped man was my fiancé, dammit, and if I don't see Mr. Dunne within the next five minutes, I'm going to raise hell so loudly you'll have the president himself down here asking questions."

"That's impossible."

"My raising that much hell? Try me."

"No. Reaching Mr. Dunne. He's gone to . . ." She caught herself. "He's unavailable."

"Okay, when Mr. Dunne makes himself available again, you tell him that I'm waiting to see him."

The girl's eyes widened. "Waiting?"

"Yes. In that chair right over there. It looks uncomfortable as hell, but I'll manage."

"But . . ."

"From now 'til doomsday, if I have to," she warned ominously. She sat down, crossed her legs, pulled a notebook from her purse, and began jotting down what she knew so far. The list was pitifully short. It was, however, long enough to impress the receptionist with the sincerity of her intentions.

"I'll try to reach Mr. Dunne," she said finally.

Amanda smiled. "I thought you might."

Jeffrey Dunne, as it turned out, was absolutely thrilled to hear from her. He would be delighted to see her. In three hours. At Donelli's place. In the meantime, would she mind very much keeping her nose out of the case? She didn't deign to respond to that. She hated to flat-out lie to an authority figure.

On the way home, Amanda stopped at Virginia's bakery for a late lunch. The small shop was empty of customers, but filled with the tantalizing aroma of cinnamon rolls. Amanda ordered three, still warm from the oven.

"You must have the metabolism of an NFL linebacker," Virginia observed as she put the plate in front of Amanda and settled across from her with her own cup of coffee. She tucked her pencil in the heavily sprayed curls in her upswept hairdo. The pencil didn't budge, balancing there like some bright yellow Japanese hair ornament. Since her hair had been tinted a fascinating shade of orange this month, it made for quite a picture.

"I only eat like this when I'm keyed up," Amanda confessed, taking a bite out of the second roll. "These are delicious, by the way."

"I suppose postponing your wedding, having the best man killed, and your fiancé disappearing would have a way of creating stress." Her expression turned sober. "Hon, how are you really? Anything I can do?"

"Not really, Virginia, but thanks for asking."

"I told you Joe and that friend of his were in here before the wedding on Saturday, didn't I?"

"Jenny Lee said you'd mentioned to her that they'd been in for your blueberry pancakes. I wanted to come, too, but Jenny Lee insisted it would be bad luck for me to see the groom. In retrospect, I'm not sure my luck could have gotten much worse."

"You know, hon, there's something else I meant to tell you about that morning. I clean forgot about it until just now. I mean it's the kind of thing that happens all the time with Jeeter, so it didn't seem important then, but now, after what happened later, well, I guess you ought to know.''

As Virginia's circuitous logic sank in, Amanda stopped eating. "What happened?"

"Well, like I said, it was Jeeter. You know how he can be, when he gets all riled up. He'd been on an all-night bender, as usual. Probably slept an hour or two over in Lacey's back room. Can't say I blame the man for not wanting to get on home. That Francie is enough to drive a man to drink. She's as looney as they come."

"Virginia!"

"Sorry. Anyway, Jeeter started mouthing off at one of my other customers, old Mr. Corbett. He's been right sick, you know. Coming here for breakfast is about the only social life the man has. Anyway, Joe and Dave finally stepped in and broke up what could have turned into a nasty fight. They cooled Jeeter off finally and insisted on taking him home. He took exception to the notion, said he was perfectly capable of driving his own pickup, but Joe was pretty adamant. They carted him right out of here, mumbling all the way about damned do-good Northerners. Joe drove Jeeter's truck. Dave followed them. You don't suppose Jeeter would go and do something crazy like blowing up that car just to get even, do you? Ever since I saw all those itty-bitty pieces of metal scattered every which way, I've been worryin' about that. Jeeter's a damn fool, but he's never been dangerous, so far as I know."

Amanda was astounded at the notion, but she was willing to entertain any theory about now. "It seems a little extreme to me," she admitted, "but I've never forgotten the time Seth Henry shot his rooster for crowing at dawn. Not much has surprised me around here since. You tell me, though. Could Jeeter have done it?"

"Well, he ain't got the sense the Lord gave a duck, but he sure has the know-how."

"What do you mean?" Amanda said, feeling her pulse race the way it always did when a hot story was beginning to come together.

"He was blowing up stuff for the highway department for years before he opened up that laundromat of his. Usually it was road beds, of course, and it's been years since he worked there, but I suspect he could have got that dynamite if he'd a mind to."

"Oh, my God," Amanda murmured. Had he raised all that fuss at last night's town meeting just to throw everyone off guard, when he'd known perfectly well that he was the guilty culprit? Was he that wily? "How do I get to Jeeter's place?"

Virginia looked worried. "Amanda, hon, don't you be going out there alone. You call Buford or Eldon to go with you. They know how to manage Jeeter."

"How do I get there, Virginia?" she repeated, glowering until Virginia backed down.

"Oh, Lordy, I hope I don't regret this. You take the highway out to the Dairy Queen, then turn right and go about a mile. There's an old red barn on the left. About a quarter mile past that, you'll see a peach orchard and just beyond that is an old dirt lane. You take that and Jeeter's place is back about a half-mile off the main road."

Amanda knew it had been too much to hope that a man like Jeeter Potts would actually live on a real street with an actual address. She jotted down the directions, grabbed her last cinnamon roll, and ran for the door.

"Amanda, I'm calling the sheriff."

"Whatever," she said.

With any luck Eldon and Buford would be too busy giving tickets at the town's four parking meters to get there before she'd had a chance to talk to Jeeter about just how angry he'd been at Dave and Donelli on Saturday.

CHAPTER

Seven

FINDING Jeeter Potts's place was a lot easier than Amanda had expected it to be—or else she was getting better at understanding the kind of directions the locals gave out. At any rate, she was there in less than a half-hour, surprised to discover that it wasn't the run-down, unpainted shed she'd envisioned. She really was going to have to work on her tendency to stereotype. The house was a small, square block, but it had a fresh coat of white paint and dark-green shutters. Two rockers sat side by side on the tiny cement stoop, hinting at a domestic harmony Amanda had no reason to believe existed. There wasn't a single barnyard animal roaming loose in the yard, which turned out to be neatly trimmed grass instead of the bare dirt she'd anticipated. Nor was there any evidence of the expected sad-eyed hound, lazing around in a patch of afternoon sunlight.

There was, however, a shotgun aimed straight at her belly.

Amanda had met Francie Potts only once before. The meeting had been considerably friendlier, possibly due to the free-flowing beer in Billy Lacey's bar during that afternoon's critical Georgia Bulldogs football game. Francie was in her early fifties. She was tall, her figure gaunt, not enhanced at all by the faded, loose-fitting yellow housedress she wore. Her face, with its high cheekbones and startlingly blue eyes, had probably been gorgeous thirty years earlier, but too much sun had turned the skin leathery and too many troubles had robbed her eyes of their brightness. Judging from the aim of her gun, however, she was still spirited and quite probably an accurate shot. After an instant of stunned silence, Amanda rallied.

"Francie," she began in her least aggressive tone. "It's me. Amanda Roberts. We met..."

"I recall," she said testily. "I ain't as big a fool as some folks like to think."

"I never meant that," Amanda said swiftly, her gaze riveted on that gun. She wondered exactly how big a hole it could blow through her at this distance. Big enough, no doubt. "Francie, do you suppose you could put that gun down?"

Francie's chin jutted up. Her gaze narrowed. "Well, now, I don't rightly see the need for that, not 'til I know what you're doing here."

"I was hoping to see Jeeter."

"What for?"

Responding to that posed an interesting quandary,

especially in light of the gun. Amanda couldn't very well announce it was because she suspected him of kidnapping Donelli or worse. She tried an indirect route.

"Francie, you know I was supposed to get married on Saturday."

"Yes'm. I heard something about that. I think maybe the *Gazette* had an item about the wedding."

"Yes, it did. Did you also hear that my fiancé disappeared before the ceremony?"

"Yes'm and I'm sorry for your trouble, but what's Jeeter got to do with that?"

Amanda phrased this next part very carefully. "It could be that he was the last person to see Joe before he vanished. He might have seen something, noticed him being followed, something like that."

Francie's expression grew even more suspicious and the finger squeezing the trigger tightened perceptibly. As a warning, it was rather effective. Amanda was torn between dashing back to the car and hightailing it back to town or standing her ground. If she took off, though, she'd never know about Donelli. She swallowed hard and met Francie Potts's scowl with an unblinking challenge of her own. She wanted desperately to dry her sweating palms on her slacks, but held perfectly still instead, waiting.

Francie's voice hardened, her demeanor fiercely protective. "You accusin' him?"

"No, of course not. I just want to talk to him to see what he knows. I'm desperate, Francie. I need to know what happened to Joe."

Apparently the emotional appeal, a woman-to-woman plea for help, reached Francie. To Amanda's relief, her trigger finger eased slightly. The barrel of the gun dipped. Now if the thing went off, it was likely to blast off a toe. Still, it was an improvement.

"Jeeter ain't here," Francie said.

"Do you expect him back soon?"

"Well, now, you never know with Jeeter. He got off work an hour back, soon as Lucille came in for the evening shift. The laundromat does its biggest business evenings, you know. Sometimes Jeeter sticks around to help out. Leastways that's what he tells me. Could be down at Lacey's with a bottle of light beer. The old fool thinks he don't get as drunk, if it's light. Anyway, that's more likely. You never know, though. He could be heading home for once. You want to sit a spell and see if he turns up?"

The prospect of sitting around and making small talk with Francie Potts and her shotgun did not excite Amanda. Besides, if she was right about Jeeter and he was down at Lacey's he'd probably be incoherent by the time he got home. And nasty tempered. The combination did not bode well for a friendly, illuminating discussion of Donelli's possible whereabouts.

"I'll catch up with him later," she said reluctantly. "Thanks, Francie."

"Be careful out there, girl. You never know who's lurking in the bushes."

"Isn't that the truth," Amanda murmured.

She waved one last time as she turned her car around

and headed back to town. She'd swing by Lacey's to see if Jeeter was there. Maybe he'd still be sober enough to talk and at least there'd be other folks around to keep him in line.

At five o'clock on a Monday night, Lacey's Bar and Grill wasn't exactly jammed. The dirt parking lot surrounding the unadorned cinder-block structure had half a dozen pickups in it, all of them with gun racks and National Rifle Association stickers. Inside, Amanda took a quick survey of the gloomy interior, which was brightened only by the flashing neon beer logo over the bar. Jeeter was not among the men hunched over their drinks. Even so, there was a chance she could pick up something about what had happened here last Friday night. She climbed on a stool and ordered a club soda. Places like Lacey's did not generally offer the kind of vintage wine she normally drank. If pressed, Lacey might be able to scrounge up a jug of near-vinegar from the back room. Amanda preferred not to press.

"So, Amanda, what brings you in here?" Lacey asked, pouring the soda and sitting the glass on one of those little cocktail napkins with cartoons and bad jokes. "Heard about what happened at your wedding on Saturday. You drownin' your sorrows?"

She lifted her glass. "With this?"

"Hey, three-fourths of the effect of alcohol is psychological, if you ask me. You want to get drunk, you can do it on a whiff of the stuff." Lacey, once the star of the local high school football team, had run this bar since the law allowed the sale of beer and wine in Morgan County back in 1971. Despite his lack of a college degree, he considered that the length of service gave him credentials as both a psychologist and a philosopher. It probably did.

"Maybe so," Amanda replied. "But for the moment I'm more interested in information than oblivion."

Lacey tensed. "What sort of information?"

"I hear Jeeter Potts was drinking pretty heavily Friday night. Was he in here?"

He glanced pointedly at the men at the other end of the bar. "I don't squeal on my customers. That's what keeps 'em coming back."

"I could have sworn it was the fact that you have the only establishment of this type in town."

He grinned and Amanda could see why he'd once been considered the town heartthrob. "That helps," he confessed.

"So, come on, Lacey. It's only a small jump from there to the conclusion that Jeeter had to have been in here."

Lacey shrugged noncommittally and studiously wiped the bar. The gleaming surface didn't need it.

She tried a different tack. "Was he drunk?"

He frowned at the blatant attempt at trickery. "I ain't even said he was in here."

"I'm taking that as a given. What kind of mood was he in?"

He scowled and for a minute she thought he wouldn't answer that either. Finally, he muttered, "You know Jeeter. You should be able to figure that out, same as you have the rest."

"Nasty?"

He avoided her gaze. "I ain't sayin' yes or no."

"Did he stick around after you'd closed up?"

"I can't serve alcohol after hours. You know the law as well as I do."

She also knew that Eldon and Buford rarely enforced it, as long as no drunken brawls broke out. Telling Lacey what she knew probably would not help her cause, however. He was already on the defensive. "I just meant did he stick around to sleep it off?"

"Maybe. Maybe not."

Amanda had talked with reluctant sources, shotgun-toting sources, and devious sources. She'd learned when to cut her losses. Billy Lacey was obviously intent on keeping whatever he knew to himself. Jeeter drank in here a lot more frequently than she did. She supposed that earned him the right to Lacey's loyalty. Even though she understood, the reticence didn't improve her mood. She slapped the money for her drink on the bar, along with an insultingly small tip. "Thanks for your help, Lacey."

He took the sarcasm exactly the way she'd intended. A fleeting expression of guilt passed over his face. She waited hopefully for a change of heart. Apparently, though, Lacey wasn't in touch with his conscience. In the end all she got for her gamble was a self-righteous glare.

"Drop in again, Amanda. Always a pleasure."

"I'm sure," she said sourly.

Thoroughly frustrated, she considered driving back to Atlanta to the office, then recalled that she was supposed to be meeting Jeffrey Dunne at Donelli's. She glanced at her watch.

"Hell and damn," she muttered. She was nearly an

hour overdue. No doubt FBI agents didn't expect to be kept waiting. She'd be lucky if he was still there. Who was she kidding? She'd be lucky if he didn't cart her in for contempt or obstructing justice or some such charge.

As it turned out, Jeffrey Dunne was a more patient man than she'd thought. He was still at the house. Inside, in fact. Amanda stood in the doorway, glowering at him as he rifled the drawers of Donelli's desk, wishing she had just five minutes with Francie Potts's shotgun to impress upon the agent the depth of her displeasure.

"Isn't breaking and entering considered a criminal offense in the FBI code?" she inquired.

Dunne turned a furious gaze on her, apparently unfazed by her irritation or her sarcasm. "One hour, Ms. Roberts. I have been waiting around for you for sixty minutes. I don't have time to play cat and mouse with you." He waved his left arm at her, apparently because it was the one on which he wore his watch.

Amanda was duly impressed with both the fancy timepiece and his ability to tell time, though not with his evasion. "Believe me, playing any kind of games with you is not tops on my agenda either. But let's not get sidetracked. What are you doing in here? I know the door was locked. I doubt you have a key or a search warrant."

"I don't need either. This is a crime scene. I figured as long as I was waiting, I might as well take another look around. I know you'd want me to be thorough."

"Absolutely," she said, smiling sweetly and trying to recall exactly where she'd left the file on Judge Price.

She was not inclined to tip her hand about that particular piece of evidence just yet. "Find anything?"

"Nothing that seemed relevant."

"I'm sorry to hear that."

"Perhaps the visit won't be a total loss, now that you're here."

"Me?"

"Yes. I'd like to ask you a few questions."

"I thought you were meeting me here to answer mine."

"In good time. First, why don't you tell me everything you know about the murder victim. I understand you knew him."

"Only casually," she said with a sigh, willing to play the game his way for the moment, if it would net her what she wanted in the end. She went through the pitifully short list of facts. "He and my fiancé grew up together. They've stayed in touch. He was here for the wedding. That about covers it. What do you know?"

He appeared startled that she'd asked. "Not much more than that," he said after a hesitation so faint she might not have noticed it if she hadn't caught the wary look in his eyes. Someone should warn him about those eyes of his. They telegraphed his moods to anyone careful enough to keep watch.

"Have you been in touch with his wife? Was she notified of his death?" Amanda asked, her gaze locked on his.

Another flicker of something, but what? All he said was a simple, "Yes."

"Then I'd like her address and phone number. I'd like to offer my sympathy. I'm sure you can understand that."

Cool green eyes scrutinized her closely. "You don't have the address?"

"It must have gotten misplaced in all the confusion. You know what wedding preparations are like."

"Actually, I don't, but I'll take your word for it."

"Can you get the information for me?"

He shrugged. "Why not? I'll give you a call."

Amanda studied his expression and decided that she could probably grow old waiting for that particular call. Jeffrey Dunne was clearly a man not in the habit of sharing. It seemed to be a genetic trait among law enforcement officers and she suspected the FBI had honed it into a talent. That didn't stop her from trying.

"Have you found out anything more about the bomb?"

"We're working on it."

"Do you think it was put together by an amateur or an expert?" she inquired, recalling what Buford had told Jenny Lee.

"I'm waiting for a report."

"Any fingerprints?"

"Some."

"Would you care to identify them?"

"We're working on it."

"What have you done to locate Joe?"

"I'm not convinced he's missing," he said and looked her straight in the eye.

The blasé response fueled Amanda's fury. "He didn't turn up for his wedding. His best friend was killed and his car blown up. His house was ransacked. There hasn't been a word from him about any of that. He was seen leaving here with another man, probably the kidnapper. Exactly what sort of evidence will you need before you decide to hunt for him?'' she demanded, fully aware of the slight widening of his eyes, but attributing it to amazement at her outburst. She continued with the uncensored version of her opinion of his work thus far. ''What the hell kind of investigation are you conducting, anyway? At the rate the FBI is moving, I'd be just as well off relying on Eldon and his guesswork to track down Donelli.''

''Look, Ms. Roberts, I can understand that you're upset,'' he began in that tone meant to placate a hysterical woman. It only sent her temper one stage further into orbit.

''Upset? You think this is upset?'' Her voice climbed as she marched up to stand toe-to-toe with him. She jabbed a finger into his solid belly. The gesture probably hurt her more than it did him. The man must spend his nights doing sit-ups by the hundreds. ''You listen to me you bureaucratic paper pusher. Joe Donelli does not walk away from trouble. If he's not here, it's because someone has kept him from being here. Now if you don't intend to find out where he is and who has him, then I'll do it on my own. I have sources. I have evidence and, by God, I've got brains, which is more than I can say for you.''

''Are you finished?'' he inquired calmly.

''Not by a long shot. The next time you want to come snooping around in my home, you get permission from me or you get a search warrant, because crime scene or not, I'll slap you with a suit that'll turn your career into a joke. Now, get out!'' She held open the door just to emphasize the message.

He didn't budge.

"Are you deaf, too?"

He actually had the audacity to smile at that. "No, contrary to what you seem to think, I have all my wits about me. I am also fully aware of your reputation, Ms. Roberts, and I'd like to offer you a little piece of advice. Stay out of my investigation or I'll slap you behind bars. From what I've observed of the journalistic profession, that might put a slight crimp into your career as well. Now, if we're through trading threats, perhaps you'd like to explain that remark about Joe being taken out of here."

In the heat of battle Amanda had mentioned what Harley Griggs had seen. "A neighbor saw him leaving right after the bomb blast. A neighbor, by the way, who has yet to be questioned by any law enforcement official."

He winced at that.

"Sort of lends credence to my claim that you're all a bunch of inept cretins, wouldn't you say?" she goaded.

"Okay. We blew it. If you're through tossing out insults, you can fill me in over dinner."

Of all the things Jeffrey Dunne might have said to her, a dinner invitation was the least expected. She stared at him, dumbstruck. "Are you out of your mind?" she asked finally.

His expression turned thoughtful. "Nope. Not clinically, anyway."

She opened her mouth to reply, then closed it as the words sank in. Jeffrey Dunne had actually made a joke. A small one, to be sure, but it had been at his own expense. And, when she looked, she realized there was a definite twinkle in his expressive eyes. Perhaps she should reevaluate her opinion. It would never do to underestimate the enemy and, despite the astonishing glint of unexpected humor in his personality, she still considered him to be an adversary. Perhaps, though, he would turn out to be a worthy opponent instead of a total jerk. Prudence suggested she go along with him.

"Dinner would be fine. Unfortunately, the diner closes at five. The nearest restaurant is a fast-food hamburger place. They have drive-through, if you're in a hurry."

He didn't even blanch. "I have time and I love their fries," he said. "How about you?"

What Amanda loved was a challenge. Jeffrey Dunne was offering that. She would willingly clog her arteries on fast food for the next month for the chance to pry any little snippet of information out of the man. She was absolutely certain, deep in her gut, that he was hiding something, probably quite a bit, in fact. Secrets, especially official secrets, were among her favorite things.

"I can't wait," she told him sincerely.

C H A P T E R

Eight

AMANDA was not surprised to discover that Jeffrey Dunne drove a government-issue four-door sedan that was only one shade darker than his gray three-piece suit. He insisted on driving. He even held the car door open for her. When she hesitated, he shook his head.

"Would you prefer it if I let you open your own doors?" he inquired, stepping aside with a mocking grin.

The pointed remark struck home. "I'm not so liberated that I'm insulted by a man's good manners. Actually, I was just wondering if it wouldn't make more sense for me to take my own car."

"Of course you were," he said, a skeptical glint in his eyes.

"It's true. You'll have to double back to bring me home."

"Your thoughtfulness is duly noted."

"But not bought?" she said ruefully. The man was far more perceptive than she'd anticipated. She was going to have to stay on her toes if she intended to pry information from him.

"Please," he corrected. "It would be rude of me to doubt a lady's integrity, wouldn't it? Rest assured that I don't mind driving. That's when I get my best thinking done. Come on, Ms. Roberts. I'm starving and I imagine you must be, too." Again, his appreciative survey of her slender figure suggested something quite different. Amanda found the purely masculine look oddly disconcerting.

If Jeffrey Dunne thought she was one of those dreary souls who wasted away in times of crisis, he was in for a rude awakening. The opposite, unfortunately, was more often the case. She'd whipped her figure into its present shape just in time for the wedding. If Donelli remained gone too long, it wouldn't last. Her three cinnamon rolls were already only a distant memory. In a spirit of defiance and in response to renewed hunger in her soul, she ordered a deluxe cheeseburger, fries and a shake and, as Dunne watched in obvious astonishment, ate every bite. Then, just to press home the point, she began stealing from his large order of fries.

When she was finished, Amanda studied the man across from her, fascinated with the prospect of discovering what made him tick. She guessed he was no more than forty. In fact, she would have pinned him as younger had it not been for the`fine lines near her eyes. She knew from jabbing him in the stomach that he was in shape. In fact, she suspected that Jeffrey Dunne maintained rigid control over every aspect of his life, which probably explained why he wasn't married. Wives and kids tended to incur disorder. On the surface, he had appeared to be a dull, by-the-book kind of guy. There was an intriguing intensity just below the surface, though. And, in the last couple of hours, she had gotten glimmers not only of humor, but of that surprising intuitiveness. It made him both attractive and dangerous.

With the enthusiasm of a journalist for any new and complex subject, Amanda set out to measure for any other hidden depths. Her practiced technique was a mixture of innocent, feminine curiosity and the finely honed skills of a seasoned investigative reporter. The combination had earned her more than her share of revelations from sources every bit as wary and difficult as Jeffrey Dunne.

Propping her chin on her hands, she said, "So, tell me, Mr. Dunne, how'd you get to be an FBI agent?"

"Are you interested in my career path or my desire?"

"The desire, by all means."

"At the risk of sounding simplistic and rather naive, I wanted to catch the bad guys."

"You could have been a cop and done that. Why the FBI?"

"Maybe it was reruns of Eliot Ness in action on 'The Untouchables.' I suffered from delusions of grandeur. I only wanted the big guys."

"And have you caught them?"

"A few," he said so modestly that she guessed it was a vast understatement. "Not nearly as many as I'd like.

You're a reporter. You know that three-fourths of what you do is tedious, mundane research, assembling facts bit by bit until you have a thorough, convincing story. It's the same for me. You think I'm being too slow and methodical, but that's the only way I know to avoid making mistakes. Do you know how many thousands of phone records and leads are checked out in a case like this? Even if I had unlimited manpower, which I don't, there's no fast way to do it. I don't want my cases to get thrown out of court on a technicality and I don't want to risk men's lives by making snap judgments.''

"Aren't there times when you put your life at risk by not making a snap judgment? While you're weighing odds, the other guy can be pulling the trigger.''

"I'm pleased you're so concerned about my safety," he said dryly. "Believe me, though, I can get up to speed in a hurry when my life is on the line.''

"What about this case? Why are you involved? The FBI doesn't turn up automatically for all bombings, does it?''

"Not ordinarily, no.''

"Then why this time? Word has it you were on the scene before anyone else.''

"I speed." He confessed it with a charming lack of remorse that appealed to Amanda's own penchant for exceeding the limits of the law by several miles per hour. It didn't keep her from noticing that he still hadn't given her a straight answer. She tried again.

"It was a Saturday evening. Didn't you have a date?''

There was laughter in his voice when he said, "Why, Ms. Roberts, are you inquiring about my social life?"

"No," she said impatiently. "I am inquiring why a man who works for the FBI in Atlanta would be first on the scene at a bombing seventy-five miles away, especially on a Saturday night when one would expect him to have better things to do."

"I just hate missing out on the action, don't you? Now, tell me about you. Journalism school, right?"

"You're evading me."

He smiled. "Yes, I am."

"Why?"

"Because I don't feel any need to explain my presence on that scene to a reporter. Take my word for it, I'm in charge. It's one of those givens in life, like death and taxes. You'll be more relaxed if you just take my presence on faith."

"I take very little at face value or on faith."

"Something they taught in journalism school?"

"And law school."

She was delighted that he seemed taken aback by her knowledge of torts and writs and rules of evidence.

"Why?" he said. "That's not a requirement for a journalist."

"My own delusions of grandeur. I wanted to go after the big guys, too. I just wanted to nail them in print with enough evidence that no court could overlook it. I figured it would help if I understood all the rules."

"How's your success rate?"

"I've done okay," she said, matching his modest tone.

"There are a few public officials serving time in jail, thanks to investigative work I've done."

"And am I right? Did you pull all the pieces together overnight?"

"No," she admitted. "It took time."

He leaned closer. "Then allow me to work this case in my own way, Ms. Roberts. I promise you I'll get results."

"In time," she qualified. She lifted her gaze to meet his and said softly, "What if Joe doesn't have time, Mr. Dunne? What then?"

His jaw tensed and his eyes turned a stormy shade. He reached across the table and took her hand, squeezing it. The unexpected gesture was surprisingly tender. It caught her completely off guard, as did his quiet intensity. "Trust me, Amanda. I really am on your side in this."

"I want to," she said. "I really do, but..." Jim Harrison's doubts about Dunne's expertise ran through her mind with disturbing clarity, followed by his determined evasiveness in responding to her legitimate questions. How could she leave Joe's fate in this man's possibly inept hands? She watched him closely as she asked, "What about the Bryan Price murder? You've had a lot of time on that."

In the blink of an eye, Dunne's friendly demeanor vanished. He sat back and studied her with a cold, disconcerting thoroughness. "Why would you ask about that particular case?"

Amanda cursed herself for playing her hand too soon. She tried to regain her advantage by skirting the truth. "I've been doing a little research for an article."

"And just when did you decide to work on this particular story?"

"Recently."

"I'm sure."

She ignored the doubting tone and plunged on. "It seems to me that there were possibilities you never even considered."

"Name them."

Oh, hell. She stared at him in silence, unable to finesse her way out of that particular fib. She'd meant to read the clippings, but she'd been distracted by more immediate research.

He sighed. "You've been talking to Detective Harrison, I assume."

"Why would you assume that?"

"His views on my investigation are well-known. He's not exactly the strong, silent type. What exactly did he tell you?"

"I haven't even confirmed that he was my source," she said, recognizing even as she spoke that she was engaging in the same sort of pointless evasiveness that she'd encountered in Billy Lacey. "Is it true or not that you spent too much time focusing on the drug angle?"

"Are you asking on the record or off?"

Amanda hesitated. At some point, she would need his comment on the record, but for now she simply wanted answers. "Off. If I need an official comment later, I'll ask you again."

He kept his gaze on her steady, apparently waiting for something. Amanda returned that penetrating gaze just as steadily. Finally he nodded, as if he'd analyzed her character and satisfied himself that she was trustworthy. "In that case, off the record, the Bryan Price murder file is very much open." He leaned closer, until she could feel the warm whisper of his breath. His tone, however, remained chilly. "And if that turns up in print, Ms. Roberts, you will be jeopardizing one of the most important investigations in Georgia in recent years. Do I make myself clear?"

The words were nothing compared to the warning in his eyes. She shuddered. This was a man with whom it could be very dangerous to tangle. "Very clear."

He nodded. "Okay. I'm trusting you with this, because everything I've learned about you tells me that you're a woman of your word. I hope you'll realize before it's too late that I'm a man of my word as well. You can trust me, Amanda. So can Joe."

"Is there a tie-in between that case and this?"

"Trust me, Amanda."

Deep in Amanda's gut, where judgments and decisions were often called, something shifted, if only slightly. "I'll hold you to that, Mr. Dunne. If you betray my faith, if anything happens to Joe, I'll come after you in print."

He smiled wearily at the thrown gauntlet. "I'm sure you will."

They were nearly out the door when Amanda caught yet another flicker of alert interest in Dunne's eyes. She turned to follow the direction of his gaze and spotted Delbert Reed and another man settling into a back booth.

From the intensity of their discussion, she doubted they were talking about the hamburgers.

"You know the mayor?" she asked Dunne.

"We've met."

"And the man with him?"

"You don't recognize him?"

She shook her head. "No. Who is he?"

"I have no idea," he said, his expression perfectly bland, though Amanda was certain he was lying through his teeth. What she couldn't imagine was why he would deny recognizing such an innocuous-looking old man, who was probably doing nothing more than complaining to Delbert about his taxes.

After Jeffrey Dunne had driven her home and left, Amanda settled in a rocker on the front porch at Donelli's to contemplate what he'd said—and hadn't said. The night was still and inky dark as clouds passed over the sliver of new moon. It had rained hard in the last hour, soaking the ground. Donelli would have been thrilled. He charted the weather with all the avidity of any farmer, cursing the dry spells, fearing the kind of droughts that had devastated the area in seasons past.

Now, though, the heavy scent of damp earth clung to the humid air. The rocker creaked rhythmically as she tried to sort through the scant pieces of the puzzle she'd assembled so far. Not one single clue was significant enough to set off a line of reasoning that would lead her to Dave's killer or tell her where to begin searching for

Joe. Though she wanted desperately to believe Dunne's promises, she knew she couldn't stand on the sidelines and wait for a break in the case. Maybe Jim Harrison was having better luck.

As she stood up to go and call the detective, she heard the faint rustling of bushes at the corner of the house. She tried to reassure herself that it was just the sound of night in the country, a stray dog, a cat, nothing more, certainly nothing ominous. Then a long shadow fell across the porch. Her pulse leapt, then raced.

"Who's there?" she demanded, wishing she hadn't been quite so quick to send the FBI agent on his way. Her own gun, which Donelli had insisted she know how to shoot, was tucked uselessly in a drawer in the kitchen. She hated the weapon and refused to carry it. Right now, with her heart thumping and a shiver of fear slithering down her spine, she rather wished she hadn't been quite so stubborn.

She peered into the inky shadows. "Dammit, who's there?"

"I heard you was looking for me," a drunken voice finally responded.

She gripped the porch rail tightly. "Jeeter, is that you?"

"Yes'm." He staggered to the foot of the steps and stood there weaving.

She felt a quick whisper of relief, then a little voice muttered a stern admonition. An intoxicated and foul-tempered Jeeter Potts could be every bit as dangerous as an unknown assailant. Amanda inched closer to the door, then had second thoughts about letting the indoor lights behind her turn her into a highly visible target.

"How about a cup of coffee?" she offered, managing a friendly, even tone.

"Never drink the stuff," he said. "Keeps me up at night." He chortled at his joke. "Now, if'n you had some whiskey, I might have a sip or two of that."

She nodded reluctantly. "I'll see what's inside. Have a seat, Jeeter."

Amanda hurried into the house, tempted to lock the door behind her. She didn't, certain she could get the drink and be back outside before the unsteady Jeeter could negotiate the steps. In the kitchen, she found a half-empty bottle of bourbon and, concerned with highway mortality, poured a scant dollop into a glass. She shook her head at the wasted effort and filled it to the rim. She guessed that Jeeter would prefer it neat and plentiful. He probably hated to water down the effects of alcohol.

Just as she was ready to go back outside, she heard the screen door open, then Jeeter's uneven footsteps as he came in search of her. A chill crept through her as she debated whether to lure him back to the porch or stay within reach of that gun. He'd looked more pitiful than threatening, but looks could be deceiving. Even so, she had just decided to try maneuvering him back outside,when he staggered into the kitchen. He dragged out a chair and sank into it, then reached greedily for the drink. She handed it to him and remained standing.

"Sit down. I don't bite." He grinned at her again,

pleased at what he no doubt considered his sophisticated repartee.

Amanda perched uneasily across from him, trying to determine if under his folds of flesh he'd once been handsome enough to entice the beauty Francie had obviously been. Even her well-trained eye wasn't able to tell. Tiny red veins had broken on his face, and his eyes, though a dark brown, seemed lost in all that puffy roundness.

"Why was you looking for me?" he asked.

"I heard you'd run into Joe on Saturday morning. I thought maybe you could help me figure out what happened to him between then and the time he was supposed to get to the church for the wedding."

Jeeter rubbed the back of his hand across his bleary, reddened eyes, then squinted at her. "Beats hell out of me. You say I saw him?"

"At the doughnut shop. Virginia says he gave you a lift home."

A slow, gap-toothed grin spread across his unshaven face. "Well, hot damn! That explains how I got there. I been wonderin' about that."

Amanda's spirits fell. "You don't recall anything about getting home that morning?"

"Nope. Last I recall I was trying to get old man Corbett to share his sports section with me. The old coot wasn't reading it, but danged if he would give it up."

"Virginia mentioned you were angry at Mr. Corbett."

He guffawed, then apparently noticed that her mood wasn't nearly as jovial. "Could have been," he admitted.

"Been told I get that way when I drink. Tried to stop it once, but decided the world didn't look so hot sober. Looks a lot better this way. Sort of like one of them Monet paintings. Pretty little things, all fuzzy pastels. Saw 'em once in Paree. Took Francie there for our honeymoon. Her daddy paid for it. Ain't been nowhere since. Suppose she holds that against me."

He leaned forward and peered at her intently. "Do you know what it said in my high school yearbook? *Most likely to succeed*. Ain't that a kick in the pants? Me and Delbert was in the same class. Nobody thought he'd make a danged thing of himself and now he's getting ready to run for the goddamned state legislature."

That was fascinating news. Amanda wondered if Delbert had actually filed and if so, why the campaign was so low-key. She hadn't realized the mayor had such grandiose political aspirations.

"You planning to vote for him?" she asked.

"Don't see why the hell not. Me and Delbert, we're like this." He tried to hold two fingers tight together, but couldn't seem to manage it. "Hard to believe, ain't it? Him being such a big shot and me being a drunken nobody. One of these days, though, that could change." He nodded. "Yes, indeedy, that could change."

"Why?"

"Because Delbert needs me to win."

"Oh?"

He wagged a finger at her. "Yep. Ain't that a kick in the pants? Like to think of myself as one of them big-shot campaign strategists. Down at the laundromat I sure can keep my finger on the pulse of things. Folks talk when they got nothing better to do than watch their clothes spin. Tell me all sorts of things.''

That said, he mumbled an apology, put his head on the table, and passed out cold. Stunned, Amanda stared at him. Tentatively, she reached over and shook him. He began snoring loudly.

Terrific, she thought, thoroughly dismayed. She had a drunken man asleep in her kitchen, a man who might be perfectly capable of wakening during the night and strangling her in bed. She could call Eldon or Buford to come and haul him home. In fact, she decided, that was the best alternative. The last thing she needed was to have Francie Potts, toting her shotgun, come over here looking for her wayward husband. They'd both end up blown to smithereens before Francie bothered to ascertain that Jeeter wasn't exactly Amanda's type.

Just as Amanda started to dial the sheriff's office, the front door flew open with a crash. She reached for the drawer in which she'd left the gun, grabbed the weapon, and pointed it just as Jenny Lee and Larry came charging into the kitchen. Eyes wide, they skidded to a halt at the sight of the gun. Jenny Lee was only momentarily daunted, however. She plunked her hands on her hips, glared at Amanda, and marched into the room like Sherman storming across Georgia. "You put that thing away right this second, Amanda Roberts! You have a lot of explaining to do."

Feeling guilty and not sure why, Amanda stuffed the gun back in its not-so-secret hiding place. "Me?"

"Yes, you." Jenny Lee seemed to notice Jeeter for the first time. She blinked rapidly, then said, "You can start by explaining why there's a drunk man asleep in your kitchen."

"That's a long story."

"We have all night, isn't that right, Larry?"

"Yes," he said, peering at Amanda intently. "Are you okay?"

"As well as can be expected under the circumstances." She gestured toward the snoring Jeeter. "He got bored with my questions."

"Then I won't disturb him with mine," Jenny Lee said. "You just march yourself into the living room and start talking. Oscar, Larry, and I have been out of our minds worrying about you."

"Why?" she said, genuinely baffled.

Jenny Lee actually looked as if she wanted to smack her. Amanda had never seen her so upset.

"Why? Why!" Jenny Lee repeated. "You left the office hours ago. You promised to come back. Nobody's seen hide nor hair of you since. When we were here an hour ago, your car was in the driveway, but you weren't home. We thought the kidnappers had taken you, too."

It took a good hour and twenty minutes to sort everything out. While Larry brewed a pot of coffee, Amanda called the sheriff to come get Jeeter. Jenny Lee gulped down an unaccustomed shot of straight bourbon and choked on it. Amanda swallowed crow as she apologized for worrying everyone. Jeeter kept right on snoring until

Eldon turned up and roused him enough to get him out of the kitchen. To the sheriff's credit, he didn't ask questions.

When things had settled down a little, Amanda tried to explain where she'd been all day. "I was just coming in here to call Jim Harrison, when Jeeter turned up," she concluded.

"Harrison's been calling all over looking for you since noon," Jenny Lee said. "His temper's almost as bad as Oscar's. He said something about dissolving your partnership if he didn't hear from you before the end of the day. Does that make any sense to you?"

Amanda glanced at the clock and winced. It was just past midnight. She felt a little like Cinderella watching her coach turn back into a pumpkin. "As a matter of fact, it does. Did he say what he wanted?" she asked as she reached for the phone.

"Just that he was losing patience. Not that he needed to tell me that. I could hear it in his voice. What did he mean about a partnership?"

"We sort of joined forces on this investigation."

Larry and Jenny Lee took in the calm announcement and stared at her in astonishment. "And they say politics makes strange bedfellows," Jenny Lee observed.

"This is one time I'll take help any place I can find it. Nobody else in authority seemed to be volunteering," she said as she dialed. The detective picked up on the first ring. At the sound of her voice, he muttered an oath that would have blistered Miss Martha's ears. It reminded Amanda of Donelli.

"Sorry," she said docilely.

"I don't want to hear *sorry*. I want to know where the hell you've been. I've been trying to reach you all day. I thought we agreed to stay in touch. If you're going to go tearing off on your own, our deal is off. I thought I made myself clear about that."

"You did," she agreed, still meek. It always worked on Oscar and even occasionally on Donelli.

"Okay. So, where have you been?"

"Spinning my wheels," she admitted, disgusted by the lack of real progress. "What about you? Were you able to get in touch with Mrs. Price?"

"Her and everyone else in the judge's family. Not a one of them spoke to Joe about investigating the case. They'd never even heard of him. As far as they know, the case is locked away in some file cabinet."

"What about your FBI sources? Anything there?"

"Nothing specific. Everyone's very tight-lipped. I couldn't even get a straight answer about the evidence found at the bombing out at Joe's. They got really nervous when I started asking about the Price case."

"Terrific." She'd been hoping to add to the privileged information she'd gotten out of Jeffrey Dunne.

"Actually, it is."

"Why?"

"It tells me something's going on."

"Detective, something is always going on with the FBI," she said with more sarcasm than he deserved. It wasn't his fault his sources were no more talkative than her own.

"Trust me, Amanda. They know something they're not telling anyone right now."

"I'm delighted they're so adept at keeping secrets, but that doesn't do us a helluva lot of good, does it?"

"As a matter of fact, it does."

"How?"

"Amanda, what's your first instinct when someone slams a door in your face?"

"To get a look behind it."

"Exactly. I think we've found the right door. All we need to do is get a look behind it."

"That's very enigmatic."

"But you know exactly what I mean, don't you?"

"Yes. As a matter of fact, I do," she said thoughtfully. The connection between the Price case and this one seemed almost a certainty, even though Jeffrey Dunne had stopped shy of admitting it. "I'll get busy on that research into Judge Price's death first thing in the morning."

"Good girl."

Normally, Amanda did not appreciate condescending pats on the head from the police. As tired and dispirited as she was tonight, though, it was nice to know that someone thought they were making progress.

"Stay in touch," he said. "And that means leaving a trail I can follow. It makes me nervous when you're out of contact."

"It makes me nervous that a hotshot Atlanta homicide investigator can't find one high-profile reporter, who isn't doing much to cover her tracks."

"Touché, Amanda. Touché."

CHAPTER

Nine

AMANDA was not looking forward to yet another discussion with Oscar about assigning her to investigate Judge Price's murder. Once he'd dug in his heels on something, he was not inclined to reevaluate. The alternative would be to ask for the vacation time she'd planned for the honeymoon. Doing that, however, would be tantamount to admitting that she didn't expect to be taking that trip with Donelli any time soon. She was a long way from wanting to concede that.

So when she walked into the *Inside Atlanta* office in the morning she braced for battle. Unfortunately, Oscar wasn't there.

"Where is he?" she asked Jenny Lee, who'd arrived moments earlier. After the previous day's debacle, she'd driven her own car from Amanda's this morning.

"I just walked in the door, too," Jenny Lee said grumpily. "Maybe he's in Joel's office."

Joel Crenshaw, the magazine's publisher, occasionally liked to have a clue about what they were up to on the editorial side. At this hour, though, he was usually at his health club working out.

"Buzz him," Amanda said.

"Amanda, I need coffee."

"You can have all the coffee you want, once I find Oscar."

"I don't suppose you ever considered buzzing Joel's office yourself," Jenny Lee said so testily that Amanda regretted not letting her take time for coffee before they left the house.

"Fine. I'll do it myself." She walked behind Jenny Lee's desk and punched in the interoffice number, then waited. No one picked up.

"Any luck?" Jenny Lee inquired more pleasantly as she returned from the newsroom, sipping on her extra-large cup of coffee. Amanda could only imagine how horrible the stuff was, since it had to have been left over from the previous day. It had tasted like battery acid then.

"No," she said. "This is really peculiar. Have you ever known Oscar to be late?"

"Amanda, it's only eight o'clock. Maybe if you hadn't insisted on leaving the house at dawn, he'd have beat us in, the way he always does."

"I suppose. Let me know the second he gets here, okay?"

"Sure. What are you going to do?"

"I'm going to tap into the data base and do a little research."

One of the biggest advantages of coming to work for

Inside Atlanta was that the new magazine had state-of-the-art equipment and an atmosphere that was almost sterile, when compared to the *Gazette*'s cluttered, dusty newsroom. In some ways Amanda missed the old gritty setting that had been like something out of the thirties, but when she needed information, there was no place she'd rather be than right here. Sitting in her own private office at her own computer terminal, she had access to news stories on file from a wide range of sources, all indexed, all available in hard copy at the push of a button.

She had barely pulled up the computerized files on the Price case and started to print them when Jenny Lee called to say that Oscar had just dragged in. "He looks beat, Amanda, and he's in one of those foul moods of his. You might want to wait before you talk to him."

Amanda appreciated the warning, but she didn't have time to wait for an improvement in Oscar's temper. Every second that passed with no word from Joe increased the horrible fear that was eating at her insides. What if he'd seen the bomber and the bomber had panicked, dragging Joe off with him? As the investigation intensified, what if the man decided he had to get rid of the one person who could tie him to the crime? The only thing that kept her from the grip of this terrifying scenario was its illogic. Surely, even a panicked murderer wouldn't take one prisoner likely to be as hard to control as Donelli. He'd have killed him on the spot, unless he had some other use for him, perhaps as a future bargaining chip.

She tapped on the open door to Oscar's office. When he didn't even look up, she walked in.

"Did you hear me tell you that you could come in?" he grumbled, rubbing his temples.

"That's never stopped me before."

"Yeah, we ought to talk about that. One of these days you need to learn who's in charge around here."

"You are, Oscar," she said dutifully.

He lifted his head and glowered at her. Amanda was more taken aback by his appearance than by his familiar scowl. He looked as if he hadn't slept in days. His complexion was an unhealthy shade of gray. He hadn't shaved. His tie was askew and if her memory served her correctly, he was still wearing the same rumpled shirt he'd had on yesterday. She pulled up a chair and sat down, ignoring his disapproving glare.

"Oscar, what on earth's wrong?"

"Who says anything's wrong?" he said, a belligerent note in his voice.

"Trust me. I'm a reporter."

"And that makes you omniscient?"

"It makes me observant. Now talk."

"Is that the finesse you use on your sources?"

"Depends on the sources. Besides, you're my friend."

"No," he said curtly. "I'm your boss. You have a bad habit of forgetting that."

Amanda stared at him, shaken by the cool rejoinder. "Oscar? This isn't like you."

"And you know everything there is to know about me, right?" He rubbed a hand across his head, further disturbing the remaining strands of gray hair. "Okay. Okay. I'm sorry. What's on your mind?"

"No," she said firmly. "You first. You look as though you could use someone to talk to."

"Dammit, Amanda, stay the hell out of my business!"

This was getting her nowhere fast. She held up her hands in a placating gesture. "Okay. Fine. As long as whatever you're hiding doesn't have anything to do with Donelli."

He stood up so quickly his chair crashed into the wall. Bracing his hands on his desk, he leaned forward. "Contrary to what you may think, young lady, the entire world does not revolve around your problems. Now get out of here, so I can think."

Stung by the rebuke, she stood up and walked toward the door. "I'm sorry as hell I bothered you," she snapped before slamming it.

"Oh, hell, Amanda," Oscar muttered. He caught her just outside the door. "Get back in here. You know I didn't mean that."

She regarded him somberly and shook her head. "Yes, you did. That's what scares me, Oscar. Something must be terribly wrong. Let me get you some coffee and we'll talk about it."

"I don't need coffee," he said, grabbing for the bottle of bourbon he kept in the bottom drawer of his desk. He poured it into a glass and drank it down. Now Amanda was really worried.

"Oscar, you're really frightening me. Start talking."

He shook his head, still stubborn. "You got enough on your mind."

"That doesn't mean I can't listen to you."

He picked up a pencil and sat tapping it against his desk until Amanda thought she'd scream. She had to bite her lower lip to keep silent while he stewed. He sighed heavily. "Actually, what I need is a favor," he admitted at last.

"Anything, you know that."

"Don't be so quick, until you know what I want."

"I said anything and I meant it."

"Actually, I wasn't going to ask, but I figure maybe it would be good for you to have something to think about besides Donelli, right?" He peered at her hopefully.

"An interesting rationalization," she observed. "Come on, Oscar. Just spit it out."

"Okay. It's an assignment, something you'll be able to really get your teeth into. I was gonna wait until after the honeymoon to ask, but since, well, since that seems to be on hold, you might as well get started. That way it'll be out of the way by the time Donelli's back, right?"

It was the last thing she'd expected and certainly the last thing she needed. She stared at him incredulously. "Now? You know I want to look into Judge Price's death."

"And I told you that was old news," he said impatiently, waving a finger under her nose. "Just this once you're going to do the story I need you to do, instead of running around independently doing whatever the hell you please."

After the initial conciliatory tone, his tone of voice had

escalated as had the color in his face. She'd never heard or seen him quite this out of control. She watched him, her own dismay increasing with every decibel. There was so much pain in his eyes, the kind of soul-deep anguish she should have noticed right away, she thought guiltily. Since Oscar wasn't likely to admit straight out that he had a problem, she supposed the only way to get a clue about what was really going on with him would be to ask about the assignment he was proposing.

"What's the story?" she inquired, forcing herself to appear meek and duly chastised. She suddenly seemed to be getting an awful lot of practice with the out-of-character technique.

"Skinheads," he said, watching closely for her reaction.

Frankly, she was shocked and there was little she could do to disguise it. If he'd suggested a splashy tabloid story on mothers who'd murdered their children, she would have been no more astonished. She was surprised he'd even heard of the kids who spouted neo-Nazi hate phrases, shaved their heads, and dressed like a cross between leather-clad bikers and guerrilla fighters.

"Why on earth would you want to do a story about skinheads? That's a little far afield for our readers, isn't it?" she began cautiously.

"I thought you liked controversy."

"Seems to me that borders on sensationalism."

"Not if you do it right," he argued. He began pacing, clearly agitated. He stopped in front of her. "For once, can't you just follow orders?" he asked plaintively.

Amanda relented, determined to hear him out. She had

promised to do anything, after all. "Okay, sit back down, Oscar. Let's hear it."

"Hear what?"

"What's behind this. You don't really want a story about a bunch of teenage racists in your magazine, do you?"

His hand raked nervously through his hair again. He avoided her gaze. "Yes."

"Because?"

"Because what?" he responded grumpily. "Because it's timely. We can't skirt a story just because it makes us sick to our stomachs."

"We do just that all the time. Talk to me, Oscar. Play it straight. When you first started talking about this, you said you needed a favor. There's a big difference between a favor and an editorial edict."

He shook his head in denial.

"Oscar, what's the angle?" She hazarded an educated guess based on his behavior. "Is it personal?"

"Leave me out of this. You just go out there and do an objective job."

"I can't very well be objective when I can see that something about this is killing you."

"Dammit, Amanda, just this once couldn't you do a damned story without questioning my judgment?"

Her eyebrows rose a telling fraction.

"Okay. Stupid question. I should have known better. You gotta keep this quiet, though. The personal stuff, that is."

She nodded. Just then Jenny Lee poked her head in the door.

Oscar scowled at the intrusion. "What do you want?"

"Do you need me for anything?"

"I'll buzz if I need you."

"Sorry. I just thought maybe I could help," she said, looking miserable and obviously feeling left out of all the commotion.

"Come on, Oscar," Amanda said.

Oscar threw up his hands. "What the hell! Come on in. Just remember this is confidential."

Jenny Lee drew herself up indignantly. "I don't gossip, Oscar."

"Ain't a woman born who doesn't gossip."

"Thank you for that glowing commendation," Amanda said. "For a man who wants our help, you're certainly going out of your way to insult us."

"Oh, good grief, don't go getting on your high horse with me. You know I think you're a damned good reporter or I wouldn't be coming to you with this.

"*This?*" Amanda reminded him pointedly.

"It's Ronnie," he said wearily. "He's gotten himself mixed up with those damned fool kids."

"Ronnie?"

"Megan's boy. My grandson." He shook his head. "Ain't that the damnedest thing you've ever heard? After all I've preached about tolerance, all the editorials I've written over the years about racial harmony and the New South and my grandkid's a goddamned racist at fifteen."

C H A P T E R

Ten

AMANDA tried to imagine Ronnie Reardon with his head shaved and racial venom spewing from his mouth. Instead, the picture that came to mind was of a gangly boy, just barely into adolescence, a crooked grin on his freckled face, a mischievous glint in his brown eyes. That boy could not have put this gut-deep fear into Oscar's eyes.

"Oscar, are you sure? Maybe he's just going through a rebellious stage. All kids his age do that. Isn't it a little extreme to label him a skinhead? Megan's felt guilty ever since she divorced his father. She's been convinced all along that depriving him of a father was some kind of a sin. You told me all that yourself. She's probably just overreacting because of the way he's dressing or something."

"No she's not. He was arrested again last night for painting Nazi symbols on a synagogue."

His voice was flat, but Amanda heard the underlying horror.

"Again?" Jenny Lee said, looking almost as shaken as Oscar. "This wasn't the first time?"

Oscar shook his head, his shoulders slumped in misery. "It seems to be the latest weekend sport with him and his pals. If the judge doesn't lock him up for it this time, I might lock him in a room and throw away the key myself." He turned anguished eyes on Amanda. "Look, I know you've got a lot on your mind right now. I'm worried sick about Joe, too. But you're the best reporter I've got."

"I'm the only reporter you've got."

"That's not true. I have a whole Rolodex filled with free lancers. Not a one of them has your instinct for the guts of a story. I want you to find out everything you can about these kids. Just how dangerous are they? Is some kind of a cult egging them on? Are they brainwashing these kids? Most of all, I want to know who the hell's behind them. I know all about that guy out west who was charged with instigating skinheads to beat to death the guy in Portland. Is there some mastermind like that here? If there's an exposé here, you'll find it. If you need to travel to get more background, I'll give you the budget."

That, from a man as tightfisted with a dollar as Oscar, told Amanda exactly how desperate he was.

"And Ronnie," she said gently. "When it comes time to run the story, is he off-limits?"

Oscar met her direct gaze. "No, Amanda. It may be the hardest thing I've ever done, but you play the story the way you see it. If you need to talk to him, I'll arrange it. Talk to Megan, too. She's scared out of her wits right now, but she'll cooperate.''

Amanda had to admit that the story intrigued her. Growing up in a well-educated, politically liberal family that was virtually blind to racial and ethnic distinctions, she'd never understood the deep-seated biases that moved others to hatred and random violence, often directed toward individuals whom they'd never even met personally. Even the turf fights between rival teen gangs were a fascinating puzzle to her. But how could she possibly concentrate on a story this complex and sensitive now? The timing couldn't have been lousier.

''Oscar, what about Joe? I can't just walk away from the search. No one else seems to be taking it seriously. The FBI seems to be pretending that he's not even missing. I keep trying to tell myself he's okay, but I won't rest until I know that for sure. I owe it to him to try to find Dave Michaels's killer, too. How can I ignore all that and give this story the attention it deserves?''

''Finding murderers is not your job,'' Oscar argued reasonably. ''You're a reporter, a professional. This is what you're being paid to do. Besides, you're better off letting the police handle Joe's case. You get too close, you could be in danger yourself. A lot of good that'll do Joe. Harrison will keep you informed and I'll stay on top of the FBI myself. We'll find Donelli for you.''

That left Amanda with three men who were all convinced they could track down her fiancé more effectively than she could. Maybe, with their greater objectivity, they could. She just wasn't crazy about relying on them. It went against the grain of her thoroughly independent nature. She felt pulled in two directions, torn by conflicting loyalties and her own frantic need for answers the FBI was not likely to hand out willingly. She tried to figure out a way to make it work.

"How about letting me have a researcher?" she suggested finally, warming to the idea. In the past, each time she'd suggested it, Oscar had balked at the expense. At the *Gazette*, he'd barely had a staff, much less what he considered frills for lazy reporters. His response had always been the journalistic equivalent of *When I was a boy, I walked five miles to school*. Now that it was in his own best interests, maybe he would go for hiring her help. It was devious, but she figured the sneakiness was for a good cause. At least he hadn't exploded, she thought, regarding him hopefully.

"For what exactly?" he said, his expression thoughtful.

"To help with the background on the skinheads, track down sources for me, you know the sort of thing I'll need. I could work the story that much faster, maybe even pull it together for the next edition."

His eyes lit up at that. Left unsaid was the fact that it would free up some of her time so she could stay on top of the car-bombing case and do some research herself into the Price killing. It wouldn't be the first time she'd juggled several stories, waiting for developments in each until one became so hot it demanded to be written.

"Who do you want?"

"Jenny Lee," she said at once. She figured Jenny Lee

would be so thrilled by the opportunity that she'd keep her mouth shut about their extracurricular investigation. Besides, Jenny Lee was developing some solid reporting instincts and shared some of the same reckless character- istics which had served Amanda well in the past. Without Donelli around to bounce her ideas off of, she needed someone. She and Jenny Lee would make a good team.

Oscar studied the twenty-three-year-old receptionist, who was sitting up boarding-school-straight on the edge of her chair, trying not to look too eager. "Who's gonna answer the phones?" he demanded.

"I'll hire a temp," Jenny Lee said at once.

"You train 'em first."

"Absolutely."

He nodded. "Okay. I suppose we can manage around the office for the time being. I'm not saying this is permanent."

"I understand," Jenny Lee said.

"And I want reports on my desk every afternoon."

"How about one of us calls in?" Amanda countered. "You don't want us wasting time on paperwork, do you?"

"Okay, okay. Call. No later than five. You understand? And remember something, these kids aren't just playing pranks. The hatred runs pretty deep and they understand all about violence and terrorism, so you be careful not to antagonize them. You get any threats along the way, I want to hear about them."

"Fine. What about a photographer? Do you want Larry on this with us?"

"From day one. Maybe he can keep you two out of trouble while he's at it."

"I'll go call him," Jenny Lee said. "When should I tell him we're starting, Amanda?"

"First thing in the morning. Tell him to come by the house at eight and we'll work out a plan."

Oscar lumbered to his feet. "Thanks, Amanda. I owe you one."

"More than that, but who's counting," she said, giving him an impulsive kiss on the cheek that left his face flaming. "Oscar, try not to worry. Ronnie will be okay."

"Say that again after you've talked to him and maybe I'll believe you."

Ronnie Reardon looked like every mother's worst nightmare.

Amanda had driven over to his high school that afternoon and waited for classes to end. She wanted to catch him off guard and without Larry around snapping pictures. Standing beside her car outside the old, dark-red brick building, she watched the students leaving in bunches, normal teenagers in jeans and T-shirts, occasional skirts and blouses. A few had cars, but this wasn't an affluent area. Most of them piled on the yellow school buses lined up in a semicircle in front of the building. She spotted Ronnie at once as he came out of the school alone. He lingered for a minute on the steps, then started toward the third bus in the line. Amanda intercepted him, stunned by the changes in his appearance.

The youthful exuberance she remembered had vanished, replaced by a sallow complexion, a faint shadow where dark-blond hair had once curled, and a dull cast to his eyes. The sleeves of his white T-shirt were rolled up. A studded black leather jacket hung jauntily over one thin shoulder. There was a tattoo on his skinny forearm. On closer inspection Amanda realized with a chill that it was a swastika.

"Hey, Ronnie," she said, plastering a friendly smile on her face.

He looked up at her suspiciously, his steps slowing. Recognition flickered in his eyes for just an instant, before his expression shut down again.

"Could we talk?"

He shook his head. "I have to catch the bus."

"I'll drop you at home. Maybe we could stop for a hamburger or something on the way."

He shrugged. "How come?" he asked finally, following her across the grass to her car. He touched the sports car with something akin to reverence and she recalled how he'd once begged her to promise that she'd let him drive it one of these days. Maybe he hadn't changed so much after all.

"I'm working on a story. I thought you might be able to help."

"Me?" Interest warred with suspicion in that single word. "What kind of story?"

Amanda didn't answer immediately, hoping his curiosity would grow. She also wanted to find an approach she could be sure wouldn't alienate him. The heavy traffic around the school at that hour gave her a natural excuse for the silence. By the time they were on the highway, she had decided to play it straight. If she didn't and he caught her, he'd never trust her enough to reveal the information she really needed. "I've been hearing some things about the skinheads around this area. Your grandfather thought you could give me the inside story."

His head snapped around and he glared at her. "So you can make us out to be a bunch of weirdos?"

She glanced across at him. "Is that what you think you are?"

His foot began to tap nervously. "No. I think we got it all right. You're the ones who don't know where it's at."

"Tell me what you mean."

He launched into a diatribe on racial supremacy that made Amanda's blood run cold. Even more chilling was the fact that he delivered the entire recitation almost by rote, as if he'd said it many times before. Biblical references abounded, used to give a shadow of respectability to the venom. He was still categorizing the enemies when they sat down in a booth. He paused only long enough to order his hamburger.

Listening to him made Amanda cringe. Hatred that ingrained could only be taught by single-minded fanatics. That it had been taught to this formerly sunny-dispositioned boy infuriated her. Oscar's concern about brainwashing took on new meaning.

Keeping her expression bland and her voice even, she asked, "How'd you meet these guys?"

"They were just around."

"Around where? School?" She couldn't recall seeing anyone else as obviously linked to the skinheads as Ronnie.

"I guess."

"Ronnie, what about that girl you brought with you to your grandfather's? Melissa?" She recalled the pretty blonde and the look of adoration on Ronnie's face when he'd looked at her. "Is she part of this same group?"

There was a faint flicker of an emotion she couldn't read in his eyes before he admitted, "No. Anyway, I don't see her anymore."

"Why not? You liked her a lot."

"She dumped me," he said flatly.

Slowly, a picture was emerging of a boy who'd lost his father in a bitter divorce and probably within months a girl he'd liked very much. No doubt he'd felt very much alone and very angry. That would have been more than enough to send an adolescent on a desperate search for acceptance. "I'm sorry. That must have hurt a lot. Is that when you met these new friends?"

"I guess."

"Could I meet them?"

His fingers drummed nervously on the table. "I don't think so."

"Why not? You know what kind of reporter I am. You know I'd be fair."

He regarded her skeptically. "You'd get all bent out of shape like Mom and Grandpa."

"No. I'd really like to hear what you all have to say."

His reluctance wavered. Obviously, he was torn between the desire to show off his new friends and new ideas and the fear that they would be ridiculed. He finally nodded. "I guess I could talk to 'em at least and see what they think."

"Thank you. Will you call and let me know when and where?" She gave him her card and scribbled Joe's phone number on the back. "I'll be at this number most of the time. If I'm not around, just leave a message on the machine."

"Okay."

"Come on. I'll give you a lift home."

"That's okay. I can get a ride from here."

"You're sure?"

"Yeah. Some kids from school are here. They'll take me."

"Okay. Then I'll wait to hear from you."

She left him still sitting in the booth, looking very much alone. She was almost at the door when he called, "Hey, Amanda."

She turned back and caught the expression of wistfulness on his face.

"Will you really let me drive your car sometime?"

For the first time since she'd picked him up at school she saw a faint glimmer of the old exuberance. She grinned at him. "The day you get your license," she promised.

"You're okay."

"Thanks, kiddo. So are you. Remember that."

On her way out of the restaurant, she stopped at a pay phone to call Jenny Lee. "Any messages?"

"Lots. None urgent. None from Joe."

Amanda swallowed her disappointment and reached automatically for one of her soothing ice-blue mint jelly beans. "How's the research going?"

"Research," Jenny Lee muttered with a disgusted sniff. "So far, I've spent the entire day trying to teach the new receptionist how to put the calls through without cutting them off. You should have heard Oscar when she disconnected his call to Joel right when he was trying to wrangle some extra space for the next edition of the magazine in case this story is ready. He was still shouting when Joel came barreling out of his office. They practically collided right here in the lobby. It took me ten minutes to calm them both down. The temp got hysterical and left. I'm waiting for a new one now."

"Well, as soon as things settle down, get those printouts in my office and go through them. You might get on-line on the computer again and see what kind of articles you can find on the skinheads. I'm sure I saw a piece in the Atlanta paper awhile back. Check the magazine listings, too. Make copies for me."

"Where are you headed now?"

"Federal court. I want to see what kind of information I can pick up on Judge Price's cases at the time of his

death. I'll check in with you later this afternoon. If
Donelli calls . . ."

"I'll beep you. You do have the beeper with you for a
change, don't you?"

"Yes, Jenny Lee. I learned my lesson the other day."

"You've said that before."

"The beeper is right here in my purse. Would you like
to call, so you can hear it?"

"No. I'll take your word for it."

"Thank you."

"Good luck at the courthouse."

The high-rise Richard Russell federal building, which
housed both the U.S. Post Office and the courts, was
downtown near the Omni. It required nerves of steel just
to weave through the maze of expressways that con-
verged on the area. She approached the dark, uninviting
garage with the same wariness she reserved for dark
alleys and Central Park at midnight. The basement metal
detectors and purse search only added to the eerie,
slightly threatening ambience. This was not a multinational
corporation with a lobby of architectural splendor. It was
dull, dreary, and functional.

It took her nearly forty-five minutes to track down
someone who could tell her what had happened to Judge
Price's cases after his death. Naturally, it was the woman
who'd been his secretary for the entire twenty years he'd
spent on the bench, first in the Atlanta courts, then in
U.S. District Court.

Mary Elizabeth Hastings appeared to be in her late
forties. There were unashamed streaks of gray in her

brown hair, which had been bluntly cut in a severe style
that would have been devastating to someone with a less
interesting face. There was a brisk efficiency to her
movements and a deep-rooted loyalty in her manner
when Amanda mentioned the judge's name. She was
discreetly reticent until Amanda showed her a press card
and told her she was conducting an investigation into the
judge's death.

Her expression turned bitter. "It's about time someone
did. The last one was a joke."

"Do you have time for a break?" Amanda asked,
sensing that it would take very little to get the secretary
to open up. "I'll buy you a cup of coffee, if there's
someplace close. I really need some help with this."

"I'll make the time. I've kept my mouth shut for too
long hoping they would come up with some answers.
Maybe you'll have better luck."

They settled for iced tea in the huge basement cafete-
ria. It was quiet at this hour. Mary Elizabeth scanned the
room and once reassured of their privacy, she shared her
frustration over the FBI's handling of the judge's murder.
"I've read a lot of testimony in court cases and sat in on
a lot of trials. I know all about the rules of evidence and
a fair amount about investigations. This whole thing
smelled from day one."

"Smelled how? Do you think there was a coverup of
some kind?"

"I'm not sure about that. I do think the work was
awfully sloppy. Dunne, do you know him?"

Amanda nodded.

"Well, he came in looking for a list of all the witnesses in the drug case. I asked him to go through the other files, but he said he'd get to it later. He wanted to run that lead first. For a while I thought maybe he was right. I mean it made sense. It was the biggest case on the judge's desk at the time and the Colombians have been known to use strong-arm tactics to make a point. There had been death threats. Take all that, add it up and what do you have? A logical case, right?"

"Sounds like it."

"Except it wasn't panning out. The Colombians were sure their guy was going to be freed anyway. I don't think they needed to kill a federal judge to make a point."

"Was the guy freed?"

"Yes, eventually. On some search and seizure technicality," she said, confirming what Amanda had heard.

"What other cases were on the judge's desk at the time?"

"Let me think now. Some kind of bitter child-custody dispute that had spilled over into abduction, an antiabortion test case, a couple of civil rights cases. Those were the most controversial, anyway."

"Any controversial enough to provide a motive for murder?"

"When you deal with issues that strike at the heart of a person's beliefs, you always have a motive for murder."

"But no one stands out?"

"Not really and, believe me, I racked my brain."

"They were all reassigned?"

"Yes."

"To the same judge."

"I'd have to check on that."

"Would you do that and get back to me? I'd like to get a look at the public record on those cases, too, once you have the list."

"I'll see what I can do to arrange it. Is tomorrow soon enough?"

"That quickly?"

"It's a couple of phone calls. I want to know who killed him, too, you know."

"We'll find out, Mary Elizabeth," she promised, hoping she wasn't overestimating her ability to accomplish what the FBI with all its manpower and access to the hard evidence had apparently failed to do. So far, though, hard legwork and persistence had untangled some fairly knotty stories for her. She'd test her intuition against formal investigative techniques any day, especially when a certain kind of close-minded male like Dunne was in charge. They had a bad habit of missing the forest for the trees. The truth, she'd discovered, was often in the middle of the forest. And, just as often, once you picked the right forest to explore, the truth was right there in plain sight. She had a hunch, obviously shared by Jim Harrison and Mary Elizabeth Hastings, that Jeffrey Dunne, despite his reassurances the other night, had gotten way off course and stayed there.

CHAPTER

Eleven

WHEN Amanda got home just as the sun was setting in a riot of orange and pink, she discovered a perfectly at home Miss Martha camped on her doorstep. The sprightly octogenarian was drinking her favorite tea from a china cup. A silver carafe, an extra cup, and a plate of sugar cookies were arranged on a damask place mat on the wicker table beside her. Apparently, she'd come prepared for a wait. Her driver was dozing inside her long black Cadillac.

"Sit down, dear," Miss Martha invited as graciously as if this were her own elegant living room. "You must be exhausted after all this running around. You really must take better care of yourself in all this heat, Amanda. You look a bit peaked."

Amanda automatically bristled at the motherly interference. "Miss Martha, you mustn't fuss over me, really." She clenched her teeth so hard they hurt. "I'm fine."

"Well, of course you are, dear. We women have always been strong. That doesn't mean we don't need to look after ourselves properly. Have some tea. I know you prefer coffee, but I'think tea is so much more soothing in times of stress, don't you?"

"Actually . . ."

"Tell me now, what did you learn at the courthouse?"

Amanda reached for the teacup, then set it back. She regarded Miss Martha suspiciously. "How did you know I'd been to the courthouse?"

Miss Martha never missed a beat. Her intelligent periwinkle eyes glistened with the purest innocence. "Why, I'm sure you mentioned it, dear."

"No."

"Oh, well, then it must have seemed a natural deduction. I do so enjoy games of logic, don't you? Of course, you do. I'm sure that's why you're such a fine reporter. So, tell me everything."

Amanda had a terrible premonition. There was no way Miss Martha could have surmised anything about a visit to the courthouse unless . . . "You hired that bodyguard, didn't you? You've been having me followed," she said indignantly.

"Please, drink your tea, dear. It's cooling off."

Amanda stood up in the faint hope that seeming taller would daunt the diminutive meddler. "I'm not drinking your tea, Miss Martha. And I am not saying one word about my visit to the courthouse until you explain how you know that's where I've been."

"Oh, all right," she said, not looking the least bit

abashed. If anything, she merely looked indulgent, as if Amanda were a sulky child, which naturally made Amanda feel like exactly that. "Of course, I've had someone looking after you. You know how impetuous you are and under the circumstances I felt I owed it to Joseph to keep an eye on you. Obviously, I couldn't do it myself. You'd spot me in no time."

She sounded disappointed. Amanda hated to burst her bubble, but this couldn't go on. "Look, I understand that you mean well, but . . ."

Miss Martha quickly interrupted the lecture she obviously did not want to hear. "Did you know that there's someone else following you as well?"

"What?" Amanda sat back down with a thump, forced to concede a certain amount of astonishment.

Miss Martha nodded triumphantly. "I thought not. See how handy this bodyguard is? My man hasn't been able to determine just who this other person is yet, but never fear, we have him under surveillance. No harm will come to you, Amanda. I assure you of that."

"I'm being followed?" Amanda couldn't quite grasp the possibility that not one, but two people were on her trail. Chances were that one of them was not on her side.

"Why, yes, dear. That's what I just said."

"By two men?"

"Amanda, dear, you really should drink your tea. You don't seem to be nearly as quick as you usually are."

Jeffrey Dunne! It could only be that damnable, smooth-talking FBI agent. He'd assigned a man to keep track of her. It was either that or the same maniac who'd taken

Joe was targeting her next. Neither option thrilled her, but there was one way to find out for certain.

"Excuse me, Miss Martha. I need to make a phone call."

"To whom?"

"I have to rid myself of a rat."

Miss Martha was on her feet at once. "Sounds intriguing," she said, following Amanda inside. She didn't even bother with her cane.

Amanda scowled at her, but didn't have the energy to fend her off. She punched in the FBI number and waited for Jeffrey Dunne to get on the line. At least this time, she didn't have to jump through hoops to reach him.

"Amanda, how are you?" he said cheerfully. "I've just been thinking about you."

She gritted her teeth at the false solicitude. She really was going to have to start that hated aerobics class again just to work off all this stress. "You muscle-bound oaf, call off your watchdog," she said and slammed down the receiver.

The phone promptly rang. It was Dunne, no doubt, ready to defend himself. She glared at it and let it ring fifteen times before she finally picked it up.

"Yes."

"I wondered how long it would be before you noticed," he said calmly. "You're good."

Amanda was not about to admit that she hadn't noticed, that it had taken her other unwanted protector to pick up on the FBI surveillance. "So you admit it," she said, deflated by the easy victory.

"Seems like a waste of energy not to. By the way, what were you doing at the courthouse?"

"Taking out a warrant to have the suspicious person following me arrested," she snapped. "Won't that be embarrassing for everyone?"

Before he could respond, she hung up on him again.

This time when the phone rang, she ignored it. She turned a smile on Miss Martha. "I believe I will have that tea now."

Miss Martha beamed. "Lovely."

After she had drunk Miss Martha's tea and sent her on her way to chew over the details of Amanda's visit to the courthouse, Amanda took a long, hot bath, wrapped herself in a thick terry-cloth robe, and settled down on the sofa to think about the case and about Ronnie Reardon. Unfortunately, she couldn't seem to keep her mind focused on either subject. Instead, images of Donelli kept tormenting her. Where was he? What was happening to him? She couldn't imagine him not checking in, unless he'd been bound and gagged.

Or worse.

The notion, once allowed to creep into her consciousness, took root and blossomed with devastating effect. She was still trembling when she heard the faint tap on the door. Pulling herself together, she tightened the belt on her robe and went to the door. "Who is it?"

"Megan Reardon, Amanda. Dad told me about the story. He said you'd want to see me."

Amanda opened the door. "Megan, you didn't have to drive clear over here. I would have come to you."

"I didn't want Ronnie to overhear us talking. He gets so upset at the least little thing. I'm sure he'd accuse me of being a traitor."

"Actually, Ronnie already knows about the story. I saw him this afternoon."

"You did? How did he react?"

"He was belligerent at first, but I think he's decided to trust me, at least for the moment."

"Thank God."

"Come on in. I was just going to put a fresh pot of coffee on. Are you hungry?"

"No," Megan said, though Amanda thought she looked as if she might faint any minute. She was determined to get some food into her. She wanted her thinking clearly as they talked about Ronnie and these skinhead friends of his.

"Here, drink this," she said, handing her a cup of coffee. "How about a ham and cheese sandwich?" she asked as she pulled the ingredients from the refrigerator.

"Really, Amanda, I'm not hungry."

"I'll fix one for you, just in case you change your mind."

As she prepared the sandwiches, Amanda studied Oscar's daughter. She was an attractive woman, despite the fact that recent tears had swollen her eyes and left her whole face puffy and splotchy. In her mid-thirties, her chin-length hair curled becomingly around a face that was normally pretty enough not to need makeup. Amanda had liked her on the few occasions when they'd met at the office or at Oscar's. She'd seemed intelligent and gutsy, a woman struggling to find her place after a nasty divorce had shattered the stability in her life. Now, though, she looked beaten by the process.

"Feeling better?" she asked finally, when Megan looked up from the coffee.

"Yes. Sorry. I know I shouldn't have barged in here tonight, but I wanted to get this over with. I feel like such a failure. How could I have let this happen to my son?"

"Blaming yourself won't do Ronnie any good. We just need to work together to find out as much as we can about these kids. Maybe we'll be able to extricate him in the process."

Megan suddenly looked more hopeful. "Do you think that's possible? He's so committed. You heard him. You must have seen it. He's not listening to reason at all."

Amanda chose her words carefully. "Ronnie's a bright kid. He's had a lot to contend with right at a time when most kids are just struggling with adolescence. He seems to have been looking for a place where he could belong. He found the wrong place, but I think he'll figure that out."

"How could he identify with them, though? For all his faults, his father's no bigot and you know about my family."

"Maybe he was just rebelling. It may only have been subconscious, a way to get even for the way his life had been disrupted."

"By the divorce."

"Maybe. I'm no psychologist. Maybe there was just a

strong personality he responded to, picking the wrong person for hero worship. When you feel like you're not fitting in, sometimes it's easier to take on the attitudes of the real outsiders. Tell me what you know about these kids. Do they go to school with him?''

''If they do, none of the other parents are admitting it. I've asked. Ronnie's counselor called me in about six weeks ago. She says he's the only one, and I can't believe they all have their heads stuck in the sand.''

''Ronnie's too young to drive, though. Where else could he have met them?''

''Who knows how kids meet? Somebody has a car and drives to the next county to a movie or to the mall. I've heard they sometimes hang out around places like that, handing out pamphlets like some of those religious sects that pester nonbelievers.''

''They print pamphlets?''

''Oh, yes. And carry signs. I'm surprised one of 'em hasn't gotten shot to death. Then, again, there are probably a lot of folks around here secretly wishing them well.''

''Even now?''

''I'm sorry to say,'' Megan said. ''Sometimes I wonder if it's like one of those cults you read about. Once you get in, you can't get out. Ronnie admitted to me once that he was unhappy with the way these kids behaved, but when he tried to back off, he was pressured into staying.''

''Pressured how?''

''I'm not sure exactly. He wouldn't tell me. I just

know that he was slowly starting to make other plans and all of a sudden he was right back in the thick of things. He wouldn't explain. I've never felt more alone or frustrated in my entire life.''

''Did you talk to his father about it?''

''Carl doesn't want to deal with problems. That's why we split up. He figured if he brought home a paycheck that was the end of his responsibility.''

''So, what did you do?''

''I tried to handle it all on my own. I especially wanted to keep it from Dad because the skinheads go against everything he believes in. But you know how Dad is. He's spent his whole life being observant. He pounces on the least little thing that doesn't ring true. It made me crazy when I was still living at home. Other kids could tell little white lies and get away with it. Not me. Dad figured out that when I fibbed, I always looked him straight in the eye. I mean that's what you're supposed to do when you're telling the truth, right? Except when I told the truth, I was usually halfway out the door or up the stairs. I only stuck around to look him in the eye when I was trying to convince him of something that wasn't true.'' She sighed wearily. ''I guess I looked him in the eye when I told him about Ronnie.''

Amanda grinned. ''Maybe it had something to do with the rather unorthodox style Ronnie's adopted.''

''That's what he said. I tried to convince him the haircut and the clothes were just a look, but Dad's no fool. He finally asked me point-blank what Ronnie'd gotten mixed up in. I gave him some evasive answer that didn't satisfy him a bit, but he let it go that time. Then Ronnie got picked up for spray-painting those hate slogans on those temples. There was no keeping that from Dad. He knows too many cops. He put two and two together and didn't like the answer. You should have heard the explosion.''

"I can imagine. How is your mother taking all this?''

"You know Mom. She's too busy playing bridge to get too worked up about it. She did mention in passing that she did not want him showing up at the country club in military fatigues. She suggested I buy him a new suit.'' She grimaced. "As if that would make a difference. I could buy him a dozen suits and it wouldn't clean up the garbage that comes out of his head these days. I read an article once by a guy who said that listening to these young kids talking that way reminded him of looking at child pornography. I know exactly what he meant.''

Amanda squeezed her hand. "We're going to get to the bottom of this, Megan. Ronnie's promised to try to set up a meeting for me with the rest of the kids.''

Megan looked terrified. "Oh, Amanda, are you sure that's a good idea?''

"It's the only way.'' She thought of her contingent of followers. "Don't worry, Megan. Nothing will happen to me.'' The FBI and Miss Martha had seen to that. For a minute Amanda was almost grateful for the interference.

C H A P T E R

Twelve

*T*HE conversation with Megan had given Amanda a renewed burst of energy and resolve. She was up at first light and settled at the kitchen table with the folder of notes Jenny Lee had brought home the night before. She was hoping for something that would give her the leverage to step up the pressure on Ronnie and assure her a meeting with the skinheads. She was looking for names, some sort of pattern to the more violent incidents, anything concrete she could go on. Instead, she found terse items about vandalism, which had apparently been relegated to the back pages of the paper. There was one lengthier story quoting parents and school officials. As Megan had warned her, all denied that there was any evidence of skinheads in their schools, yet there were photographs taken on a nearby street as skinheads passed out their hate literature.

The scanty and inconclusive reporting was both good

news and bad. It meant her story would be breaking new ground. It also meant that she had to start from square one with Ronnie. Fortunately, it was still early enough that she could catch him before he left for school.

"We need to talk," she said, making sure he realized it wasn't a mere request. "With your friends."

"I . . . I haven't been able to set it up yet. I mean, it's not like they have office hours or something."

Amanda bit back her temper. "Ronnie, it really is important."

"I'm not so sure they're gonna want to talk to the Commie press in the first place."

"*The Commie press?* How dare you say that about something your grandfather pours his heart and soul into," she snapped before she could stop herself. Antagonizing him wouldn't help.

"He's just like all the others," he retorted sullenly. "The media's all run by a bunch of liberal kikes."

If Ronnie had been standing in front of her, she would have smacked him into the next county. Instead, she swallowed back the bile stinging her throat and repeated, "The meeting's important. Set it up for after school. You can talk them into it, Ronnie. Just tell 'em how many people they'll be able to reach with their ideas if they do this interview. I'll throw in hamburgers. If they hate the media as much as you say, they ought to like being fed at our expense."

"They won't see you someplace like that."

"Where then?"

"Out on the old highway, near Jeeter's place. You know where that is?"

"I've been there."

"It's the next turnoff. There's an old shack. We meet there sometimes. It's not like a clubhouse, so don't go getting any ideas about snooping around. You won't like what we do to people who betray us."

The veiled threat would have sounded melodramatic if he hadn't sounded so deadly sincere. Amanda kept her voice perfectly neutral. "I'll be there. I want the kid who's in charge, Ronnie. The spokesman. Okay?"

"I said I'd try." He hung up on her, leaving her to wonder why he'd been so insistent on meeting at such an out-of-the-way place. Surely, he wasn't setting a trap for her. It was a disconcerting prospect, especially since there was no way she could back out of the meeting. She could practically hear Donelli shouting in her ear to do just that. Words like *reckless* and *impulsive* came to mind.

Fortunately, before they could have much impact, the phone rang again. When she answered it, no one spoke, but she could hear breathing on the other end of the line. "Who's there?" she demanded.

"Is this Ms. Roberts?" a slightly familiar feminine voice inquired nervously. Everyone today seemed terrified by the prospect of talking to her. Was it her technique or was it, perhaps, that none of them had anything pleasant to say?

"Yes. Who is this?"

There was another long hesitation. "This is Francie, Ms. Roberts. Francie Potts."

"What's wrong, Francie?"

"I don't know if I should be calling you 'bout this. Jeeter'll probably have my hide, but tell the truth I'm scared."

"Why?"

The question was met with silence.

"I won't say anything," Amanda reassured her.

Francie gave a dry cackle at that. "You won't have to, hon. Once I tell you, I guarantee all hell's gonna break loose. You won't be able to stop it."

Amanda sensed that whatever courage Francie had gathered in order to make the call was fading rapidly. "Listen, Francie, I'm heading out your way in a few hours anyway. Why don't I stop by?"

The response was a *click,* then dead silence.

Amanda suddenly worried that waiting until this afternoon was not such a terrific idea. She grabbed her purse, a reassuring handful of jelly beans, and her notebook. She woke Jenny Lee, who stared at her groggily.

"Amanda, it's still dark out," she grumbled.

"It is not dark. The shades are still drawn. Now, listen to me. I'm going out to Jeeter's, then to a meeting with Ronnie. Hopefully, by the time I'm done, I'll have a fix on Oscar's problem. If you can reach Larry, tell him to meet me there. Can you remember that?"

"I'm not stupid, Amanda."

"No, but you are half asleep."

Jenny Lee scowled at her. "What if Jeffrey Dunne calls looking for you? What should I tell him?"

"He won't call," she said dryly. "He'll know exactly where I am."

Jenny Lee seemed to struggle over her meaning. "I don't get it."

"Never mind."

"What about Jim Harrison?"

"Take a number. I'll get back to him tonight."

"Amanda, you know how upset he gets when he can't locate you."

"He'll survive."

"What about me? What should I do?"

"Give Mary Elizabeth Hastings a call at the courthouse and see how she's coming with those files. Here's the number. I'd like to take a look at 'em late this afternoon or tomorrow morning, if she's managed to locate which judges have them."

"Maybe I could do that."

Amanda hesitated. She'd never trusted anyone else to ferret out such critical facts for her. What if Jenny Lee missed something important? On the other hand, she could understand her desire to be given responsibility, maybe even a chance to come up with a sidebar story on which Oscar would give Jenny Lee her first byline. Amanda remembered the exhilaration she'd felt the first time she'd seen her own name above an article. It had been an inconsequential story for her college newspaper, but she'd immediately felt a depth of satisfaction and pride that almost nothing else matched.

"That's a possibility," she said finally, unable to flat-out deny Jenny Lee her first shot at a break. "Let's see how our schedules work out."

As she drove the twisting, mist-shrouded back roads, she found herself automatically tuning the radio to Donelli's favorite country-music station. At once she felt closer to him, recalling all the times they'd battled over his musical preference. Hell, they'd battled over almost everything, including her work and the danger it sometimes put her in. Yet he'd always known deep down that she could never give it up. It was who she was. She had been miserable without it when she'd first moved to Georgia. It had filled up all the empty hours when Mack had left and it could again if Donelli didn't . . . She slammed the door on the frightening thought before it could take over again and drain her of the energy she needed. She would need all her wits about her today if she was to first cajole Francie Potts into talking and then wheedle information from Ronnie's reluctant cohorts.

Francie was waiting for her on the front steps, thankfully without her shotgun.

"I wish you hadn't come," she said miserably, clutching a sweater around her thin shoulders. "I shouldn't never have called you."

"Something was obviously on your mind, Francie. Let's sit and talk about it."

A stubborn glint came into her eyes. "Don't need to sit. Don't want to talk."

"Did Jeeter do something?"

''No,'' she said so rapidly and so adamantly that Amanda was sure she was lying.

''What did he do, Francie?''

''I said it ain't got nothing to do with Jeeter.''

''Then why are you so scared to tell me about it?''

She fidgeted with a thread so persistently, it threatened to unravel the whole damn sweater. ''Because it don't look good.''

''You mean it could make him look guilty of something?''

She nodded.

''What?''

Francie swallowed hard and twisted that thread around and around her finger.

''Francie? Are you scared of him?''

''He's a miserable, lying old drunk, but I ain't scared of him.''

''Then why can't you tell me?''

''Because it won't stop with you. I realized that the second I called. I tell you and the first thing you know half the cops in Georgia will be swarming all over the place.'' As if that required further explanation, she added, ''I like my privacy. It's nice and quiet out here. Jeeter leaves me be. I don't want no trouble.'' She sounded plaintive. She glanced at Amanda, then away and sighed. ''But if it's as bad as I think, then I got a duty. Isn't that right?''

''I can't answer that if I don't know what you're talking about,'' Amanda said, reaching the limits of her patience. She was just considering throwing in the towel when Francie drew in a deep breath. Apparently

responding to some sudden and totally inexplicable
switch in inner direction, she said, "I guess there ain't
no choice. Jeeter's made his bed. I guess he's just
gonna have to lie in it this time 'cause he ain't gonna
make me crawl in there with him. You might's well
follow me."

She led Amanda around in back of the house. A
chain-link fence surrounded a yard that was every bit as
tidy as the front. Azalea bushes bloomed along the back,
spilling a profusion of pink and purple blossoms across
the landscape. An out-of-control forsythia bush sent branches
of yellow tangling with the fence. Francie skirted the
yard and headed toward the woods. Amanda followed,
but with slightly less enthusiasm.

Amanda had never been exactly an outdoorsman. She'd
fallen into a patch of poison ivy on her first Girl Scout
camping trip and had never gone near the woods again.
Trailing into the Georgia backwoods with a woman
who was comfortable toting a shotgun—even though
she was without it at the moment—ranked somewhere
relatively far behind camping. She went anyway, her
senses attuned to every snap of a branch, every whisper of a leaf.

They had walked for about a half-mile, when Francie
stopped at the edge of a clearing and pointed to a small
shack. Unpainted, rough-hewn boards had been fashioned
into a sturdy little structure about the size of a garden
shed. It if hadn't been sitting in the middle of nowhere,
that's exactly what Amanda would have assumed it was.
An impressive padlock dangled loose on the front door.

Suddenly, a prickle of fear crept across the back of her neck.

"Francie, what is this exactly?"

"Jeeter makes moonshine out here."

Amanda stared at her. "Liquor? He makes his own liquor out here?" She could have sworn he got more than enough beer at Lacey's bar without making his own stock.

As if she'd read her mind, Francie said, "Old habits die hard. Jeeter's granddaddy made moonshine when it was dry in these parts. His daddy did the same, just 'cause he was too cheap to buy the other. Jeeter's never really got the hang of it, but he comes out here and messes around for old times sake."

"Is it because moonshine's illegal that you were afraid to bring me here?"

Francie looked disgusted. "You see any need for me to show you an old still?"

"No."

"Then don't be askin' foolish questions. Get on over there and take a look. Lessen you're dumber than I thought, you'll catch on."

Amanda crept closer to the shed, uncertain exactly why she was approaching it with such trepidation. Of course, it was just big enough to hold someone who'd been bound and gagged. Suddenly she couldn't move fast enough. She yanked the padlock off and tossed it aside, then tried to open the door. It was jammed, the wood swollen from the recent rains.

"Joe? Are you in there?" she said, pushing against the door with her full weight.

Francie gave her another disgusted look and lifted the door a fraction on its warped frame. It swung open. Inside the gloomy interior all Amanda could see was the odd, cobweb-draped apparatus that was apparently Jeeter's infrequently used still. Her gaze swept every corner of the small room, but there was no sign of Joe or anyone else. Her hopes dashed, she turned to Francie. "What?"

"Over there," she said, pointing to a lumpy burlap bag in the far corner, but making no move to lead the way.

Amanda hesitated, sensing a trap for the second time that morning. Finally, telling herself that she was becoming totally paranoid, she crossed the threshold and stepped inside. She stopped again, waiting for the dreaded sound of the door being slammed closed, locking her in this dark, damp place. All she heard, though, was the utter stillness of the woods, the faint rasp of Francie's breathing, and the roar of her own pulse pounding in her ears.

It was her own natural curiosity which propelled her the rest of the way into the room. She poked at the burlap bag with her foot, hoping no snake would come slithering out. Behind her she heard another of Francie's dry chuckles.

"It ain't gonna bite. Open it."

She bent down, tugged at the burlap, then peered inside. Her eyes widened.

"Oh, my God," she whispered, turning back to Francie. "Dynamite."

"Look at the rest," the other woman insisted.

Bits of wire, duct tape, and what looked like the inner workings of a clock. Amanda was certainly no expert, but it all seemed to add up to one thing: a bomb. Buford's guess about the amateur, makeshift construction of the bomb used to blow up Joe's car came back to her.

Francie was right. In the next half-hour, the cops would be swarming all over this place.

CHAPTER

Thirteen

*J*IM Harrison, Jeffrey Dunne, and Eldon Mason were having a territorial dispute. All three claimed the newly discovered evidence belonged to them. However, they didn't seem anxious to take possession. They had surrounded the dynamite so cautiously Amanda wondered if they feared it might be set to explode.

"Gentlemen, I can assure you that the burlap contains only parts, not a finished product," she said. "Otherwise, both Francie and I would have been blown to bits long before you arrived."

"I still want the bomb squad to examine it before we mess around with it," Harrison said patiently.

"So do I," Jeffrey said.

Amanda had a hunch they were not referring to the same bomb squad. Eldon looked as if he felt left out, since he had no bomb squad of his own, unless Buford's Vietnam experience qualified him. He nudged the bag with his boot, watching it with much the same expression of caution on his face as she imagined had been on her own earlier. Since she already knew the outcome, she couldn't think of a single reason to stick around.

"Fine. You all battle it out. I have other things to do," Amanda said, turning away.

"Hold it," Dunne said.

Though she was sorely tempted to ignore him, the absolute command in his voice brought her to a reluctant halt. No doubt he was masterful at intimidating suspects. She supposed as job skills went, it was a good one for an FBI agent to have. Since as far as she knew she wasn't under suspicion of any crime, it only infuriated her. She waited, deliberately tapping her foot impatiently.

His gaze clashed with hers. "What *things* do you have to do that are more important than this?" he demanded. "What the hell were you doing out here, anyway?"

"I was invited," she retorted. "How about you? I called the sheriff. I don't recall making any mention of the FBI."

"These days we're a package deal."

"How comforting."

Dunne scowled at her. He seemed more inclined to shake her, but apparently another of his skills was keeping a lid on his temper. "You still haven't answered my question," he reminded her. "What brought you snooping around on Jeeter's property?"

Amanda refused to look at Francie, who was standing as far away as she could get, as if distance alone would keep her out of this mess. "I received a tip. Let's leave it at that."

Dunne's eyes turned that fascinating stormy shade again. "Don't start waving that protecting-my-source crap in my face," he warned.

"Why not? Some of us do live by a code of ethics."

"You know, Amanda, considering that smart mouth of yours, I'm amazed Donelli hasn't made a scarecrow of you and strung you up in that garden of his to fend off the blackbirds."

Unreasonably stung by the observation, her expression turned rueful. "No doubt he's considered it."

"And?"

"We reached an understanding."

"God help him," Dunne said, shaking his head.

"I hope so, since the FBI seems uninterested in his whereabouts."

Dunne rubbed his hand over the short bristles of his hair. "Dammit, Amanda, can't you give it a rest for ten minutes?"

"No."

"Don't you want to stick around and find out how the dynamite got here?"

"I'm sure your superior intelligence will come up with an answer to that and pass it along to me when the time is right," she said, unwilling to admit that she would give her eyeteeth to be around when they questioned Jeeter. With any luck, however, maybe she could get to him before they did. Irritating Dunne sufficiently might hasten her departure. At the moment he appeared to be slowly counting to ten.

Before he reached the end of the count and his rope, Harrison stepped between them. It was not the first time she had noticed his perfect timing. Anticipating backing, she was not prepared for him to say sternly, "Okay, you two, back to your corners. Let's try to make some sense of this, instead of casting aspersions on each other."

She stared at him in amazement. "Since when did you become the sweet voice of reason in all this?"

He regarded Dunne with apparent dislike and muttered, "Let's just say I've been impressed with the importance of cooperation on this case."

"I'm thrilled for all of you, then," Amanda snapped, indignant that the whole damn law enforcement universe seemed to be conspiring, while she grappled alone. Normally, she preferred it just that way, so apparently it was just the attitude that had put her in such a sour mood.

"I'm getting back to work," she announced. All of a sudden no one seemed particularly interested. That might have hurt her feelings if she'd taken it personally. She attributed it, instead, to the fortuitous arrival of the two bomb squads.

She slipped away from the crowd and made her way to the nervous Francie. "Francie, how did you come across the dynamite?"

"I didn't, leastways not first thing."

"Then Jeeter found it and showed it to you."

"Not exactly that, either. He came out here night

before last. Didn't stay long, though. Not like usual. Came back looking real upset. Right in the middle of *Jeopardy*, it was. I remember, because they were asking the big final question and I had to hush him up, so's I could hear the answer. Once that cute Alex Trebek said good night, I took a good look at Jeeter and saw he was practically white as a ghost. Wouldn't say a word about what was wrong, when I asked. It gave me a terrible start. For a minute there, I thought maybe he'd come across a body out in the woods or something. Or maybe he was having one of them heart spells he has every now and again. He said no, though. Said he was just fine.''

"What did you do then?"

"Do? What's to do? When a man says everything's just fine, you ever known him to admit different right off? I waited to see what would happen. Didn't seem no better last night, so first thing this morning I came out here and took a look for myself.''

"Why do you suppose Jeeter didn't just get rid of the bag? He could have taken it off in the woods and buried it or dumped it in the river. That's what a guilty man would have done.''

The concept seemed to surprise Francie. "Why, yes, ma'am. I suppose you're right. You think Jeeter's innocent?"

"What do you think?"

"Either that or he's a bigger fool than he ever gave me reason to believe." She sounded a little disappointed. "What are you gonna do now?"

"See if I can track him down. I suppose he's at the laundromat."

"Should be. Could be on his way home for lunch. Sometimes he does that, just so I'll have to fix it for him. He knows I watch my soaps right then."

It sounded as if Jeeter had a mean streak, but that didn't mean the man would turn violent. Still, Amanda wanted to be the first to see his reaction to the discovery of the dynamite. She was still willing to give him the benefit of the doubt. He struck her as too wily to leave the stuff right where it could be traced to him. The police were likely to be less open-minded. In fact, most cops of her acquaintance—Donelli included, in his least attractive moments—were more than willing to accept the obvious, especially if that meant clearing a file off their cluttered desks. Jeeter had access to dynamite from his days with the highway department. Dynamite and other telltale materials were found hidden in Jeeter's shed. Ergo, Jeeter blew up Donelli's car. Except, of course, that as far as she knew he had no motive. Not even she could stretch the argument they had over Jeeter's driving home drunk into a motive for violent retaliation.

With most of the local cops out at Jeeter's she was able to hightail it into town at top speed. She found Jeeter counting out quarters into neat little stacks. When she spoke to him, his already shaky hand knocked them all back down.

"You here to do laundry?" he asked, peering hopefully for some sign of dirty clothes.

"Nope. I came for some answers."

His reddened eyes narrowed. "What about?"

"How'd the dynamite get on your property, Jeeter? Did you put it there?"

"Ah, shit," he muttered and rubbed his hand across his unshaven face. "How'd you find it?"

"That doesn't matter. Did you put it there?"

"Do the cops know?"

"They're probably right behind me. Come on, Jeeter. Tell me what you know. Maybe I can help. Did you put it there?"

"Hell, no. What kind of danged fool do you take me for? I found it the day after that explosion. I knew how it would look. I was gonna get rid of it, but I figured the way my luck runs, I'd get caught and that'd look even worse. I figured it was safe enough for a day or two, 'til I could figure things out. Nobody goes out to that old still anymore. They know I stopped making moonshine years ago. I shoulda just called Eldon right off, but I ain't used to turning to cops for help."

"Who else knows about that still?"

"I suppose most everyone who knew about my daddy and granddaddy has an idea it's out there somewhere. Ain't nobody been there, so far as I know."

That did nothing to narrow the field. There was, however, one group of people who had access to the property: Ronnie Reardon and his cohorts. It was too early for her appointment with them, but that would give her more time to take a look around before they got there. It was going to be fascinating to discover which of them knew about Jeeter's little moonshine operation.

* * *

The road Ronnie had told Amanda to take was little more than a cleared stretch of red clay, filled with muddy ruts and lined on both sides by dense woods. The trees seemed to close around her as she progressed, shutting out the sun and stirring old fears. She tried to guess exactly how near to Jeeter's property the winding road was taking her, but in no time she lost all sense of direction. With the ensuing sense of isolation came increasing nervousness. The distant sound of a dog barking and an answering howl suddenly reminded her of all those prison escape movies in which hounds tracked the bad guys through woods just like these. It gave her the creeps.

Was she making a dreadful mistake in coming to this out-of-the-way spot without telling anyone the specific location? All she'd given Jenny Lee was her basic agenda. What if those bodyguards she resented, but somehow counted on, really had lost track of her? She hadn't spotted either of them all day. She trusted Oscar's grandson, despite his misguided affiliation, but what of the others? From all she'd learned they were more than capable of violence. Once again the gun Donelli had insisted she have was safe at home.

What had passed for a road came to a sudden and unexpected end. Amanda turned off the engine and sat there, debating how to proceed. A faint prickle of alarm hit, just as her door was yanked open, nearly tumbling her from the front seat. She jerked around and met the fiercest gaze she'd ever seen. Red-rimmed, the brown eyes pinned her in place, her breath lodged in her throat.

Suddenly, the boy laughed, a wild, disconcerting sound that sent a chill down her spine. "Thought you said she was tough," he said over his shoulder to someone just out of Amanda's line of vision.

"There's guys in prison because of her," Ronnie Reardon said, sounding defensive. "Grandpa says she's the best reporter he's ever seen."

"And that makes her tough? Jeez, Reardon, you are such a jerk." He turned back to Amanda, a smirk on his face. "Come on, lady. I hear you want to talk."

"We could talk here."

"That wouldn't be polite," he mocked. "My mama told me you should be hospitable to outsiders. You are one of them liberal, Northeastern types, aren't you? Guess that qualifies you for a little taste of our Southern hospitality. Gotta wonder about your manners, though. Reardon here said you wouldn't be coming until later. Were you hoping to take a look around the place before we arrived? No need for that. I'll show you anything you want to see." He leered, hopefully just to unnerve her.

Amanda sensed a surprisingly adept intellect behind the crude and menacing facade. She decided it would be a mistake to underestimate this adolescent, who still had pimples on his narrow, pinched face. She evaded his inquiry about her early arrival, but did tell him, "My politics and birthplace aren't the issue here. I'm a reporter. I'm trained to be objective."

"We'll see," he muttered. "Follow me."

Ronnie caught Amanda's gaze and flashed a warning. She didn't need it. She recognized a treacherous minefield when she stumbled into one. Everything about this young man's coiled intensity and deep-seated anger spelled danger. She also felt the bruising strength in his hand when he clamped it around her wrist and dragged her along behind him.

No more than a hundred yards from where they'd left her car, they came to a clearing only slightly deeper than the one which hid Jeeter's still. A one-room cabin that would have been perfectly suited to a national park sat in the middle. Unlike tourist cabins, however, this one had an unusual decor. Bright red graffiti adorned the outside, all of it was inflammatory and all of it was painted with exquisite care. Amanda shuddered at the sight of the bold swastika that served as the centerpiece. Her escort turned and grinned at her apparent discomfort.

"You like our artwork?" he inquired, leading her into a sparsely furnished room with similar decor. "Ronnie here's real good with a paintbrush, if you need anything done over at your place."

"Thanks, but I prefer wallpaper."

"Yeah, I suppose you would, being such a high-class type and all." He went to a cooler, drew out a beer, and held it up. "Want one?"

"Sure," Amanda said. As breakfast or lunch it lacked the prescribed nutrients. As a friendly gesture, she figured accepting it was the only way to go. Maybe he wouldn't notice that she didn't actually drink the stuff.

He popped open two cans, then pulled up a chair to

face her. While he sipped on the beer and watched her, Amanda took her time studying him as well. He appeared to be no more than eighteen, maybe twenty. He was dressed in green military camouflage gear and steel-toed boots, all ready for his own personal war. His head had been shaved, probably about ten days ago, judging from the dark shadow growing back. His complexion was pale, the way it gets when someone prowls mostly at night or hides out in caves. About five-ten, his neck was thick, his shoulders and upper arms were well muscled, and his hands were broad and callused. They looked as if they could snap a thick branch—or even a fragile neck— in two. Coupled with the just plain mean look in his eyes, his hands were deeply disturbing.

"So, what do you want to know?" he said finally.

"How about your name?"

He considered the question, apparently giving it far more importance than she'd ascribed to it. "Reginald," he said, rolling it slowly off his tongue. He giggled. "Yeah, I like that. Re-gi-nald. Sounds high-class, like one of your snooty friends, don't you think?"

Countering the intended insult, Amanda nodded agreeably, but said, "I think it sounds phony. Try again."

He raised his hands in mock dismay. "And blow my cover?"

"I thought you liked attention."

"I'm a generous man. I prefer to share it with my associates."

"You mean you like to keep the heat off yourself. I wonder why. Would it embarrass your family?"

"Hell, no. My old man's a big shot . . ." He choked off the statement, momentarily looking like a guilty kid. "Forget I said that."

Amanda seized the unexpected opening, knowing it was risky. She could lose him. However, if she let him control the interview, filling the air with his vile beliefs, she wasn't sure she'd be able to stomach it long enough to get what she was after. "Forget what?" she said. "That your father is an important man in the Aryan movement?"

He blinked rapidly, but that was the only indication that she'd hit the mark first time out. "I never said . . ."

Amanda smiled. "You didn't have to."

His defiant demeanor slipped back into place, like a mask pulled down to hide the truth. "Put it in print and I'll sue you for slander."

She shrugged indifferently. "Then I'll just have to prove it's true. Shouldn't be too hard."

"It will be if you don't know who my daddy is."

"But you'll have to reveal that to take the case to court, won't you?"

He jerked his gaze up to clash with hers. The antagonism held, then slid away. He grinned suddenly and gave her an admiring thumbs up. "Okay, so we played that one to a draw."

Amanda shook her head. "Uh-huh. I won. Care to try for another round?"

He leaned back and tilted the can of beer up to drain the last drop. "Why not?" he said, his manner offhand, though she sensed a growing tension just beneath the surface, a faint awareness that he might not be quite the hotshot he'd imagined himself to be. Even so, Amanda counted on his deeply ingrained arrogance to propel him on. "I ain't got nothing better to do this afternoon than drink beer and play word games." He popped open another beer just to prove the point.

"Try this one: dynamite."

He nodded. "Good word. Who was that actor used to say that on TV all the time? Jimmy? J-J? Can't remember. Anyway, what about it?"

"You know how to get your hands on any?"

"I suppose I could. What do you need it for?"

"Proof."

"Of what?"

She chose the direct route. "That you blew up my fiancé's car. What I don't know is why."

He was shaking his head before the words were out of her mouth. "No way, sugar. Bombing's not my style."

"But you do have access to the dynamite, don't you?"

He ignored that and asked, "Why the hell would I want to blow up your old man's car?"

She was winging it now. "Maybe because he was investigating you?"

"Look, sugar, let's get a few things straight here. You taking notes now?" He stared pointedly at the still-empty page of her notebook and she realized that he'd been toying with her after all, perhaps even trying to see exactly what she knew. She'd underestimated him. It was the kind of careless mistake that could get her killed.

"I'm taking notes," she confirmed, pencil poised.

"Okay, then. I ain't crazy about niggers or Jews. I think it's about time we white folks reclaimed this country, got rid of all them job quotas and crazy civil rights rules designed to protect the minorities. Majority rule, ain't that what democracy is all about? Are we clear on all that?"

"Perfectly." She managed to say it without shuddering.

"As for the rest, as far as I know, your old man ain't done a thing to get on my bad side. I'd have no reason to go after him."

"Even if he was digging into your affairs and finding some things that would make your life uncomfortable?" Now that she'd raised the possibility, she could see it would make sense.

"What's he gonna find? I got busted a few times for destruction of private property, desecrating a few temples. So what? That's all a matter of public record and I ain't ashamed to admit it. It ain't likely to hurt me at my place of employment, if that's what you're getting at." He grinned, just in case she hadn't gotten the humor. "I'm an independent contractor, so to speak. Folks I work for know who I am and what I do. I got to get the message out any way I know how. At least I wasn't the one who slugged Geraldo Rivera on national television, though I most certainly sent a thank-you note to the guy who did."

Amanda tried another tack. "Who else might have had access to Jeeter Potts's still?"

The seemingly out-of-the-blue question clearly startled him. "What's an old still got to do with anything? I thought Jeeter abandoned that place once he discovered you could buy bourbon a lot faster and cheaper.''

Amanda noted that he knew at once the place she was talking about. Unfortunately, she also recognized that his failure to hide that knowledge probably meant he didn't understand its significance. There wasn't so much as a flicker of guile in those brown eyes burning into her, just unabashed curiosity and the faint edge of ever-present hostility. She sighed and answered him, willing to trade information with the devil himself if it would lead her to Joe.

"We just found extra dynamite and other material that could have been used to make the bomb over at Jeeter's place. Have you seen anybody else out here in the last week or so? It could have been somebody you see around all the time or somebody who didn't belong. I'm not sure which.''

Her still-unidentified source suddenly looked nervous. He shook his head, but Amanda was certain he was lying through his perfect teeth. She turned to Ronnie, who continued to hover near the door. "How about you?''

He glanced quickly at his leader, then shook his head. "I ain't around here that much.''

"Look," said his buddy. "I'm not admitting to anything, but if you ask me, the Federal Bureau of Investigation is getting exactly what it deserves for coming around here and messin' in things that ain't any of their business.''

"You've gone up against Jeffrey Dunne a lot?''

He shook his head impatiently. "Not Dunne. He's just a front man. Everybody who needs to know knows his gig. I'm talking about the guy who was sneaking around undercover like some kind of superspy.''

Amanda was thoroughly confused. ''Who?''

''You know. The guy who was offed in that bombing.'' He turned to Ronnie. ''What was his name, Reardon?''

''Michaels. Dave Michaels.''

She stared, aghast at the implication. ''What are you talking about? Dave Michaels was Donelli's best friend. He was down here for our wedding.''

''I don't know nothing about no wedding, but I do know that your pal Dave worked for the government. Check it out, Ms. Hotshot Reporter. See how the FBI feels about losing one of their own. I don't know too much about journalism, but it sure seems to me that's your story.''

It suddenly seemed that way to Amanda, too.

C H A P T E R

Fourteen

*T*HE tires on Amanda's car sent mud flying as she spun back onto the highway en route to Jeeter's. She was going to take Jeffrey Dunne apart limb from limb and enjoy every minute of it. The prospect of boiling him in oil held a certain primitive appeal.

Unfortunately, when she had bounced over the deeply rutted land to Jeeter's for the second time that day, she found the driveway empty. Francie poked her head out the door.

"You ain't too popular with those men about now," she commented. "Takin' off the way you did seemed to upset them." Her lips twitched in a hint that she found the idea of distressing the law particularly pleasing.

"The feeling is mutual," Amanda said. "Did they come to any conclusions after I'd left?"

"None that made a bit of sense to me."

199

Amanda stared at her, puzzled by her apparent lack of panic. "They don't blame Jeeter for the dynamite?"

"No, ma'am. Now I ask you, does that make a bit of sense? Jeeter turned up an hour or so after you took off and they questioned him a little, sorta like they just felt they oughta, then they left. Jeeter went off, madder than an old wet hen about my meddling."

She seemed philosophical enough about it. Her chin jutted up with a touch of defiance. "He'll settle down after a while, I suppose, especially when he realizes they ain't gonna come after him for that still."

"I think they have more on their minds than a little moonshine."

"You, for instance?" she said with surprising cunning.

Amanda sighed. "I suppose so."

Her attack on Jeffrey Dunne would have to wait a bit. She was sure she could work up a good head of steam in a day or two, just as easily as she could this afternoon. Donelli would be proud. It was one of the few times in her life she'd actually allowed patience to overrule her impetuousness.

"Francie, could I use your phone a minute? It's long-distance, but I'll charge it to my credit card."

"Help yourself," she said, standing aside. "The phone's over there by the lounger."

Amanda went and perched on the edge of the big, lumpy chair that had obviously molded itself to Jeeter's girth. She called Jenny Lee.

"What's happening at the courthouse?"

"Mary Elizabeth found the files. She'll stick around there until I call her back. What should I tell her?"

"That you'll be over as soon as you can get there and that I'll get there before they close the place down for the night."

"You mean it?" she said ecstatically. "You're really gonna let me help?"

"I said I would."

"Thanks, Amanda. I won't let you and Joe down, I promise. By the way, Larry's fit to be tied because he can't find you. He says Francie aimed a shotgun at him when he turned up there."

Amanda found herself grinning as she imagined the encounter. Now that she'd spent a little time with Francie, she had a feeling the older woman wasn't nearly as crazy as she'd been made out to be. She'd just adopted a pose and decided she liked the effect.

"Tell Larry I'm sorry I missed him. You might send him back out this way. Tell him there's an old shed just up the road from Jeeter's I'd like some pictures of." She gave Jenny Lee the directions. "Warn him to approach the place cautiously. I'm not so sure the natives there are friendly."

"Huh?"

"Just warn him."

"Speaking of warnings, half of the law enforcement types in Georgia seem to be hot on your trail."

"I'm not surprised."

"You haven't murdered anyone, have you?"

"So far, I'm only considering it."

Jenny Lee gasped. "Good heavens, Amanda, I was only teasing. No wonder Miss Martha's in such a dither worrying about you. You shouldn't talk like that."

"What does Miss Martha have to do with this?"

"It seems you got away from her bodyguard."

Good Lord, unless Jeffrey Dunne's pal had stayed with her trail, she had been in there with those two skinheads alone. She would have been a whole lot more terrified if she'd realized that. She shuddered at the thought of what could have happened. "I didn't mean to, believe me. Apparently, he got distracted by all the commotion at Jeeter's."

"So, where should I tell him you are now?"

"He's there?"

"Sitting across from me and watching me like a hawk. It is very disconcerting." Her voice dropped. "Actually, he's kinda cute, if you like the type. All brawn and a killer smile."

"Don't let Larry hear you say that."

"Why not? A little competition might shake him up some."

"I think Larry is sufficiently bemused by you."

"Do you really?" she said hopefully. "I mean I think he is, too, but it's so hard to tell. What makes you think he's hooked?"

"Jenny Lee!"

"Oh, yes. Sorry. What should I do with this guy?"

"Give him a break and tell him to trail along with you to the courthouse. He might as well earn his keep.

Besides, I don't envy anyone having to tell Miss Martha that they've screwed up. I'll see you both as soon as I can get there."

"Actually, unless you're in a real rush, you might want to poke your head in here first."

"How come?"

"Oscar's got a visitor, that guy the mayor assigned to head up his citizens' crime commission."

"George Tolliver? What's he doing there?"

"Beats me, but Oscar is beginning to look apoplectic."

Amanda groaned. "I'm on my way."

Amanda was used to Oscar's rages. But while he enjoyed shouting matches with his staff, he never, ever yelled at anyone outside of his own little family of employees. It occasionally made Amanda yearn to be an outsider.

At any rate, she couldn't begin to imagine what the mayor's minion could have said to draw Oscar into a fight. She just hoped she could get back and calm things down before Joel Crenshaw came breezing into the newsroom and exerted his considerable clout as publisher to settle the argument by firing his editor for costing them a subscriber.

George Tolliver was sweating. Amanda took one look at the man appointed by the mayor to help investigate Dave's death and Joe's disappearance and decided he had obviously wandered into the middle of something that was way over his head. He and Oscar were still engaged in an apparent shouting match. It was impossible to tell exactly what they were saying, but the windows in Oscar's office were not nearly thick enough to disguise the heated tone.

Amanda debated intruding, decided there was more to gain than to lose, and stepped inside. Oscar never even glanced at her. His furious gaze was riveted on George Tolliver, who turned a look of sheer desperation on Amanda.

"She'll understand," he said hopefully.

"Don't be so sure of that," Oscar retorted. "When it comes to the First Amendment, Amanda's right on track with the guys who drafted it."

"What seems to be the problem?" she inquired, smiling at George Tolliver with encouragement. With the desperation of a drowning man, he snatched at the lifeline she'd thrown.

"I . . . I was just explaining to Oscar here that it wouldn't . . . wouldn't be in the best interests of this area to have some big article coming out about those radicals." His face was flushed and his collar was so tight, she was afraid his head would explode like a balloon blown up too far.

"Radicals?" she repeated with exaggerated innocence. She sensed at once where this was heading. What she couldn't begin to imagine was why a man like George Tolliver would be concerned with an exposé of the area's youthful racists.

"Skinheads," he confirmed, wrinkling his nose with apparent distaste.

"I see. You want us to drop the story. Why?"

"Image. We don't want our image to be linked...linked to folks like that, not now when we're just beginning to...to emerge as one of the most vital areas of the South. Why, Atlanta's playing host to...the Olympics. How would it look if just a few miles away there were these...these hooligans?"

"A few miles away there are these hooligans," she pointed out, trying not to become distracted by the hitch in his speech pattern.

"But you don't have to *say so*," he said urgently.

"In other words, you expect *Inside Atlanta* to lie?"

" 'Twouldn't be a lie. No, ma'am. I'm not asking you to say they aren't here. Just don't say...don't say anything at all."

Amanda smiled. Oscar sat back, rested his hands on his stomach, and watched with obvious relish as she asked, "You're known hereabouts as a religious man, aren't you, Mr. Tolliver?" She cursed herself for the hint of drawl that seemed to creep into her voice every time she had to deal with heavy accents for more than ten minutes of polite conversation.

Tolliver was nodding. "Of course. I'm a deacon in the church. Head...head of the building committee, too. Everyone knows that."

"That's right. Your good deeds are well known in these parts. Since you're so active, I'm very sure you've heard of the sin of omission." Amanda was a little shaky on the seven deadly sins, but hoped she could make this sound right up there with them. "Seems to me that it can be every bit as evil and certainly every bit as illegal as actually doing something wrong, don't you agree?''

He squirmed miserably. Apparently, Seth Hawkins's sermons on hellfire and eternal damnation had been extremely effective. ''Well, now...''

She interrupted. ''As a journalist, it's my obligation to tell the truth. The whole truth, that is, not just the part that suits me.''

His beady little eyes narrowed into slits as he tried to figure out just where she was heading with this. ''You're saying you won't back away from this?'' he guessed, tugging frantically on the knot in his tie. When it was loosened, he opened his collar.

She shook her head sorrowfully. ''I really don't see how I can.''

''But Delbert says...''

''Yes,'' she said, instantly on the alert. She did so love it when people invoked authority figures in the course of a previously mild-mannered threat. ''What does the mayor say? I should think he'd want to rid the community of these hatemongers.''

Tolliver blinked. ''Why, of course he does. Goes without saying.''

''May I quote you on his behalf? You are acting as his spokesman on this, am I right?''

''Yes, but...'' He swallowed hard and ran a finger around the collar of his shirt, then tugged another button free. ''Actually, I think you'd best be talking to Delbert directly. I don't... don't want to go putting words in the man's mouth, not on a sensitive topic like this.''

Amanda nodded. "I see your point."

"And you'll call him directly?"

"When the time is right."

"Then I'd best be going."

"I'm delighted we were able to reach an understanding, Mr. Tolliver," Amanda said.

He appeared bemused, but relieved to leave. "Yes, naturally. Want to cooperate with the media. That's why I came."

"I'm sure."

When he'd gone, Oscar chuckled. "Nice work, Amanda. Old Tolliver still hasn't figured out exactly what happened in here."

"I just have one question."

"Oh?"

"How the hell did George Tolliver discover we were working on a story about skinheads?"

"An interesting point, Amanda. I'm sure you'll find out."

"You're damned right I will," she said.

She was almost through the door when Oscar called her. "By the way, Amanda, if you go out to the *Gazette* and snoop through the files, you may find some interesting information about our friend Tolliver."

"Save me the time, Oscar. What information?"

"George Tolliver at one time headed up the Ku Klux Klan in these parts."

As bombshells went, it was a doozy. Amanda's mouth dropped open. "Him? In the KKK? I thought he was the epitome of respectability."

"You're in the South, Amanda. The two concepts are not mutually exclusive. Look at that Duke fellow over in Louisiana. A former KKK Grand Dragon. Says he reformed, but all he did was learn to sugarcoat the hatred. Lot of folks thought he was fine enough to be in the U.S. Congress. Almost stole the damn election with his respectable racism.''

Skinheads. The Ku Klux Klan. What on earth had she gotten herself into, Amanda wondered as she went back to her desk. She felt as if she'd stepped back decades in time. The Klan had been formed by a small group of disgruntled Confederate soldiers in Tennessee after the Civil War, men who'd continued to cling to an old order and used their beliefs to spread hatred and terror. Images of cross burnings and white-robed men sent a chill down her spine. Those images had been resurrected in mainstream politics when David Duke had run for the Senate in 1990. His opponents had used old newsreel footage of the Louisiana politician in front of a burning cross to demonstrate his past allegiances. Now he was even hinting around that he'd like to run for president.

What was the link between the local Klan and the skinheads, though? Was it simply their shared racist attitudes? Was this the youth movement of the KKK under a different label? She pulled out the new batch of clippings Jenny Lee had found for her. In the files, she found evidence of a loose alliance. Nationally, the attention-grabbing skinheads were thought by some old-timers to be a means for getting their ideas back into the spotlight.

Amanda tried to imagine George Tolliver in his tailored suits and wingtip shoes having anything in common with young people like Ronnie Reardon. Her imagination failed her, but she knew better than to rely on appearances alone. She couldn't envision him in a white robe and hood either yet, according to Oscar, he at one time had favored that attire.

One thing was for certain, it appeared Tolliver had unwittingly supplied her with her first clue that these young racist rebels might not be acting entirely on their own. Now what she needed to know was the connection between them and Dave's death. The skinheads might not have been behind it, but they sure seemed to be delighted about it.

As she drove across town to the Richard Russell federal building to meet Jenny Lee, Amanda tried to sort through the clues that were suddenly emerging at a more respectable pace. Discovering that Dave Michaels might be an FBI agent put things into a different perspective. If Ronnie's friend was right about Dave, if he was here undercover on a controversial investigation, it was entirely likely that he, not Joe, had been the actual target of the bomb. And it seemed to make sense that it had something to do with the skinheads or the local Klan or both. The threads were all coming together, but she couldn't quite detect the final pattern.

Since an awful lot seemed to hinge on Dave's actual occupation, she turned into the first gas station she spotted and called Washington information for the FBI's number. When she was connected, she asked for agent David Michaels.

"I'm sorry, we have no one by that name listed."

"In D.C. or at the agency?"

"We have no one by that name listed."

She considered trying the same call to the Atlanta office, but decided word would get to Jeffrey Dunne all too quickly that someone had made that particular inquiry. It wouldn't take him long to add two and two and come up with the means to muzzle her until his investigation was neatly concluded.

Exactly what, though, was Jeffrey Dunne investigating? It had to be more than Dave's murder. That file with the clippings about Judge Price and Dunne's own admission that the Price murder case was still open suggested that this trip to the federal courthouse was definitely a start in the right direction.

When Amanda identified herself to security, the guard sent her to a conference room. Mary Elizabeth Hastings, Jenny Lee, and a hulking man who could only have been her own misplaced bodyguard were settled around a long table stacked high with boxes.

"Good heavens," she murmured, daunted by the task ahead of them.

"It's not so bad," Mary Elizabeth said. "Actually, I'm still hunting for a couple of files. I figured this ought to get you started."

"God bless the Freedom of Information Act." She

looked closely at Mary Elizabeth. "All of this is public record, isn't it?"

The secretary nodded. "If you have the patience to wade through it, it's yours. Anything that didn't come out in open court wouldn't be kept with these particular files."

"We were just talking about what we ought to be looking for," Jenny Lee said. "Any ideas?"

"A murderer. Of course, most likely, that won't be what the case is all about. The case, though, will have stakes big enough that it's worth murdering a judge to affect the outcome."

"We're talking federal court here," her bodyguard commented. "The stakes are not likely to be rinky-dink."

"Look, if this were easy, the FBI would have figured it out."

He seemed to share her skepticism on that point, too, but he nodded, plucked an incongruously small pair of reading glasses from his pocket, and chose a file. Jenny Lee took her files to a chair on the opposite side of the conference table and went to work, too. Assured that they were settled, Mary Elizabeth excused herself.

"I'll stop back a little later," she said. "There's a phone if you need to call me."

"Thanks for everything."

"I just hope you find what you need."

Amanda began with the drug case that had been the focus of the FBI probe. She wanted to determine why they'd been so convinced that the dealer was behind Price's murder. After an hour of reading testimony and

court documents, Amanda had to agree with Detective
Harrison. Even at the time of the murder, before the drug
case was concluded, it was apparent that the dealer was
likely to be freed on a technicality. There were legal
questions of improper search and seizure and lack of
probable cause that would no doubt have forced Price's
hand. In the end, in fact, the case had been dismissed by
another judge.

Amanda had not been overly impressed with Jeffrey
Dunne at the start and he irritated the daylights out of her
now, but she was sure he was too savvy to spin his
wheels in such a wasted effort. Had the drug case tie-in
been simply a smoke screen for the FBI's real investigation? Which of these cases was so sensitive that the
agency had wanted to keep a lid on it? Amanda reached
for another file.

The next one was a vicious child custody dispute in
which the mother had skipped with her two-year-old
daughter despite court orders regarding the father's rights
of visitation. She'd been charged with kidnapping. The
grandmother had been held in contempt for refusing to
reveal her daughter's whereabouts. Judge Price had actually thrown the elderly woman in jail for a time. Had that
been enough to trigger his murder? Amanda knew emo-
tions ran high in such cases, but that high? She couldn't
imagine it. Besides, even though the custody dispute was
ongoing and charges of kidnapping were now pending, it
did not seem likely to be something in which Dave
Michaels would be involved on an undercover basis as

the skinhead leader had suggested. She put the file aside and reached for another one just as Jenny Lee gasped.

Amanda went to peer over her shoulder. "What?"

"Right here. I'm surprised Oscar didn't think of it. He had to know about it. It happened right here in his own backyard."

"Oscar's mind is on other things these days. Let me see."

The case involved an Anti-Defamation League suit against the local chamber of commerce. According to the testimony and enough documents to fill several boxes, the chamber had been systematically making it difficult for Jewish-owned businesses to open or, having achieved that, to succeed in the small community east of Atlanta. Deposition upon deposition indicated that commercial rents were boosted whenever it was apparent that a new business had Jewish ownership. Business licenses and certificates of occupancy were held up for months. Systematic harassment designed to frustrate and finally intimidate occurred with such regularity that there was little doubt about it being a concerted campaign.

The case against the chamber of commerce had been thrown out by a local judge, who should have removed himself from the case because of his own close ties to the chamber. The federal civil rights suit had been scheduled to begin before Judge Price for one week after his murder. Everything in his past record indicated he would rule in favor of the plaintiffs.

"Look here," Jenny Lee said. "See who was president of the chamber of commerce then."

"Who?"

"Henry Lucas."

"Well, I'll be. How come he's not in jail?"

"There's been a whole bunch of continuances, according to this. It's back on the docket next month."

Amanda was fascinated by the idea of the chamber president as murderer. "Keep looking," she told Jenny Lee, grabbing her purse. "There could be something else."

"Where are you going?"

"To have a chat with Mr. Lucas. Meet me at Joe's later." The bodyguard appeared suitably grateful for the clue. He ambled out after her.

She found the chamber president in his real estate office. In his gray seersucker suit, red suspenders, and matching tie, he looked like a prosperous plantation owner. The only thing missing was a straw hat to sit atop his thick white hair.

"Sit down. Sit down," he said. "What can I offer you? I have a spot of bourbon here, if you fancy a drink. I know this must be a trying time for you. Mighty trying."

"I could say the same for you," she said.

"Not me. Business is booming in town. Booming. Just sold the Foley place. You know the one over on Miller. Big old antebellum. Needs a little work, but these folks'll do it up right. No question about that. Now what can I do for you?"

"Actually, I was hoping you could help out a friend of mine," she said, improvising.

"Sure thing. Somebody moving to town? We have a few right nice properties available."

"I was thinking of commercial property. My friend is considering leaving New York. She has a lovely boutique up there, but you know what life is like in New York these days. She'll be here in a few days on vacation and thought she'd look around. I noticed that there's a space available right on the main road into town. I think it's where old Mr. Foley had his insurance company, in fact. Since he retired down to Florida and sold out last winter, you must be anxious to get that rented."

"Absolutely. I think we could work out a nice deal. You just have your friend come right in here. I'll see that she gets the royal treatment. What's that name now? I'll make a note on my calendar."

"Myrna," she said. "Myrna Silverberg. She'll be so grateful."

Henry Lucas's jovial expression faltered. "Yes. You send her on in," he said, but his tone was a shade less enthusiastic and the gaze he directed at Amanda was speculative. "Don't suppose she'd be happier in Atlanta. I mean if she's used to big city ways and all, don't you think she'd want more action than she's likely to find in our little town?"

"Actually, I think a slower pace is precisely what she's looking for and I've told her what lovely people live out this way. She's very anxious to meet all of you. Perhaps at the country club. Oscar's thinking of hosting a little gathering there." That ought to send the club management into a tailspin. Henry Lucas appeared flustered enough.

"Yes, well," he mumbled halfheartedly. "I'll be looking forward to it. Yes, indeed."

Amanda beamed at him. "You've been so helpful, Mr. Lucas."

"Any time, my dear. Any time."

Amanda suspected the generous sentiment was considerably less sincere than hers had been.

CHAPTER

Fifteen

*I*F luck was finally on her side, Amanda figured her visit to Henry Lucas would precipitate some sort of action. She had a feeling she was within a hairsbreadth of understanding the connection between the skinheads, the Klan, and possibly Joe's disappearance, but she couldn't quite tie everything neatly together. She hoped Henry Lucas's next step would give her another clue.

She glanced around until her gaze fell on Miss Martha's bodyguard, who was trying to look inconspicuous. He was about as successful as a bodybuilder hiding out in a roomful of kindergartners. She strolled over, clearly disconcerting him with her direct approach. He jammed his hands in the pockets of his slacks and watched her warily.

"Mr. . . ?"

"Carmody. Ken Carmody."

"Mr. Carmody, I'm hoping I've stirred up a hornet's

nest," she said cheerfully. He didn't appear nearly as thrilled as she was. "Come now. I wouldn't want you to be bored."

"Ms. Roberts, I haven't been bored since the day I started all this. I must say, though, that I pity that poor guy who hooked up with you. You're a real handful."

"Actually, that guy isn't hooked up with me yet," she reminded him. "But I intend to see that he is the very second Henry Lucas leads me to him."

"You think he actually knows where your fiancé is?"

"If he doesn't, I'd bet money that he knows who does," she said. "Shall we hang around and keep an eye on him?"

"Whatever you say. My instructions are to stick to you like glue."

"Do you happen to have a car phone in there?"

He held open the door to his very fancy car. "All the modern conveniences."

"Really? I don't suppose you have any of those little long-range tracking devices, the kind you plant under the hood of a suspect's car."

That killer smile Jenny Lee had mentioned spread across his face. "Afraid not."

"Too bad," she said, getting into the car and picking up the phone. She called Miss Martha, who snatched up the phone on the first ring.

"Is that you, Kenny?"

Kenny, Amanda thought, glancing at the hulking form leaning casually against the front bumper, his gaze riveted on Henry Lucas's office. "No, Miss Martha, it's Amanda."

"Oh, my dear, where are you? I've been worried sick ever since Kenny said you'd vanished."

"He told you?"

"Well, of course he told me. Do you honestly expect my nephew to hide things from me?"

"He's your nephew?"

"Yes, dear. Isn't he a lovely boy? I believe he works out at a gym, though when he has the time I can't imagine. Pediatricians do work so hard."

Amanda's gaze shot back to her bodyguard. She tried to imagine those huge hands ministering to a tiny baby. She found herself smiling, albeit weakly, at the image. "You hired a pediatrician to watch out for me?" she said, not even wanting to consider what Donelli would have to say about the logic in that.

"Well, I'm not actually paying him, if that's what you mean. When I explained the problem, Kenny was more than willing to help out. He had to give up a fishing trip, but I promised to make it up to him."

"But what if there had been trouble, Miss Martha? We could both have been killed."

"No need to worry about that. Kenny's quite a good shot. I taught him myself."

Good Lord. Miss Martha would never cease to amaze her.

"Okay, never mind," Amanda said, deciding a quick change of subject was definitely in order. "Actually, I called to find out what you know about Henry Lucas."

"Henry? Why? What's he gone and done now?"

Amanda detected a suggestion that Henry had a penchant for getting himself into jams. "So, there is something," she said. "Has he been in trouble before?"

"There was that unfortunate trouble with the chamber of commerce a few years back. I don't believe it's been resolved yet, but Henry took the blame. I suppose he had to, being president of the chamber and all, but I never believed for a minute it was his idea."

"Why not?"

"You have to understand what it's been like around here for the last thirty years or so. Change has come rapidly in the way folks think, the way they're expected to behave. Too rapidly for some. I'm not saying the changes aren't right, mind you, just that it's been difficult for some to accept them. The ones who've held out have been driven underground. They're not quite so open about their feelings, but that doesn't mean they've changed down deep. Henry's caught in the middle. He knows what's right, but he's had his friends to consider. He's a loyal man."

"Are you saying you think he was the scapegoat for someone else?"

"It's the only thing that ever made a bit of sense to me."

"Thanks, Miss Martha. I'll stay in touch," she said, her mind already piecing this new information with what she already knew. Just then Ken Carmody tapped on the window and nodded toward the opposite side of the street. Henry Lucas was just getting into his car.

"Let's follow him," she said at once, starting for her own car.

"I don't suppose I could talk you into just coming along with me," the doctor said with a certain wistfulness. Apparently trying to keep tabs on her was wearing on him.

"Sorry. I work best alone."

He shrugged. "Whatever you say. I'll be in the vicinity, though."

"I'll be counting on it."

By the time she got her car started, Henry Lucas was already a block away. She squealed out of her parking place, made a U-turn, and went after him. Keeping him in sight without being seen herself was a lot trickier than the movies made it appear. Then again, movies rarely tracked people over twisting country roads, when traffic that could serve as a decoy was virtually nonexistent. She was stiff with tension by the time he pulled to a stop in the driveway of a small house in Madison. A couple with two toddlers met him halfway up the walk. He took a set of keys from his pocket and led them inside. Only then did Amanda notice the For Sale sign in the yard. Terrific! Unless those kids had been dragged along for the perfect cover, the man was showing real estate.

Henry Lucas showed the same family three more houses before he finally called it a night about nine and went home. Amanda was exhausted and hungry and thoroughly frustrated. She wasn't quite willing to relinquish him as a suspect yet, despite Miss Martha's thoughtful defense. There was something about their conversation, though, that nagged at her, some hint she should have picked up on at once.

Loyalty! The word had surfaced a lot, not only in connection with Henry Lucas, but with George Tolliver as well. Both men were extraordinarily loyal to the same man: Delbert Reed. Miss Martha herself had described Tolliver as one of Delbert's toadies. And he'd certainly bustled down to *Inside Atlanta* in a hurry to try to stop that story on the skinheads. Was there a connection? Nothing she'd found so far linked the mayor in any way with the skinheads, the Klan, or the Price murder, though that didn't mean the link didn't exist.

On her way back to Donelli's she picked up a copy of the *Gazette* just for something to read before bed. All those high school football scores were like a narcotic. Combined with the quilting circle activities, they were enough to knock her right out for the night.

As soon as she got home she checked for messages from Jenny Lee, then changed into jeans and one of Donelli's T-shirts. His scent still lingered on the soft cotton, which made her feel closer to him. For the first time since this whole terrible ordeal had begun, she felt as if she really had a chance to find him. If Henry Lucas was feeling trapped, it was entirely possible he would do something crazy, something that would point the way straight to the mayor and to her missing fiancé.

She fixed a sandwich, poured herself a glass of apple juice, and took the late snack out on the porch along with the stack of mail that had accumulated during the last few days. She sorted through the congratulatory wedding cards and bills and was about to toss the whole batch aside when she started thinking about the phone bill. If Joe's call to Dave Michaels was on that bill, she would finally have his home number. A talk with his wife could go a long way toward resolving some of her questions about the murder victim.

Ripping open the envelope, she scanned the long-distance charges for some sign of an unfamiliar number. There were calls to Joe's parents, calls to her own family, and at least two dozen to the *Inside Atlanta* office. Not one of the calls listed was to an unfamiliar out-of-state number. She was about to conclude that Joe hadn't made that call from the house when she recognized the Atlanta number for the FBI. It was listed not just once, but half a dozen times, starting at least three weeks before the wedding. The last call had been made the previous Saturday at 4:45 P.M. Dear God! That call had been made within minutes of the bomb explosion.

Stunned, Amanda tried to fit this new piece into the puzzle. Joe had called the FBI, most likely to report the bombing! No wonder they'd been on the scene so quickly. Obviously, he'd known about Dave's connection to the agency. Maybe he'd even been aware of Dave's undercover investigation. For all she knew, Dave might have been in Georgia for months. Hell, judging from the number of calls, Joe could have been working with him.

Once considered, the possibility that Joe had been working in some sort of loose alliance with the FBI began to make a crazy kind of sense. Amanda was still wrestling with the notion that he had kept something that important from her, when a car turned into the driveway. She saw the headlights long before she heard the motor. The thought of Ken Carmody off lurking in the bushes was very reassuring.

Minutes later, she heard a car door slam and saw a woman crossing toward her. She recognized Oscar's daughter.

"Megan? What are you doing here?"

"I need to talk to you." She stood at the foot of the steps, her hands dangling at her sides, her expression hesitant. She looked as if she were uncertain of her welcome.

Puzzled by Megan's wariness, Amanda turned cautious as well. "Okay," she said slowly. "What's going on?"

"Ronnie says you had that meeting today."

"Yes. It went just fine. I think the pieces of this are beginning to come together. I learned a few other things today as well that have almost convinced me these kids aren't acting alone. In fact, I'm almost certain I know who's behind them."

Expecting Megan to be pleased, she wasn't prepared for her to say, "I want you to drop it, Amanda."

"Megan, you know I can't do that. Why would you even want me to?"

"Because if anything happened to you, I'd never forgive myself for getting you involved."

The catch in Megan's voice convinced Amanda she was serious. "You didn't. Your father did. There's no reason for you to panic now, just when we're getting close to the truth."

"Amanda, please. Just look what happened to Joe."

Amanda felt her heart still. "Joe? What does he have to do with this? What exactly do you know that you haven't told me before, Megan?"

"I don't actually know anything. It's just that it's all my fault that Joe was kidnapped. It has to be."

"How on earth is that your fault?"

"I hired him, Amanda. I asked him to find out about these skinheads. I told you I'd tried to handle it on my own before Dad found out. Well, I hired Joe. I hadn't really paid him anything yet," she said in a rush, the words tumbling out. "I don't even know how much an investigation like that costs. Joe said we could work it out later. I was so embarrassed. He promised me, though, that he wouldn't say anything to you or to Dad. I should never have made him promise that. If you'd known, maybe you could have prevented the kidnapping."

Amanda felt an irrational fury building inside. She knew that Megan was wrong. There was nothing she might have done to prevent what happened, not if Dave Michaels was in the thick of the investigation as well. Still, if Megan hadn't set the wheels in motion . . . She sighed. There was no point at all in thinking that way now.

"Please, forgive me, Amanda. Please."

"Megan, it really isn't your fault. You were protecting your son. Joe's a professional. He knew the risks."

"But . . ."

"No. No buts."

"You'll stay out of it now, won't you? Please."

"I can't, Megan. I have more reason than ever to find the truth."

After Megan had gone, exhaustion nearly overwhelmed Amanda. Too tired even to leave the porch, she picked up the local weekly newspaper she'd brought home earlier. She glanced over the headlines on the front page, then turned inside. At the top of page two was a picture taken at a fund-raiser for Delbert Reed the previous Sunday, the day after her aborted wedding. She read the cutline about his candidacy for the state legislature, then glanced back up at the picture. Suddenly, her breath seemed to lodge in her lungs.

"Oh, my God," she whispered, staring at the family portrait. There with Reed were his wife, his two daughters, and his son. Unless Amanda was wildly mistaken—and the way the *Gazette*'s print smeared it was entirely possible—Delbert Reed's son Leroy looked an awful lot like Ronnie Reardon's skinhead leader. He was wearing a suit and tie instead of fatigues, but that couldn't disguise the cropped hairstyle or the cold, calculating eyes she remembered so well.

She jumped up so fast she sent her apple juice tumbling onto the porch. Everything clicked neatly into place at last. Suddenly, she understood how George Tolliver had found out about the story on skinheads. No doubt Leroy had mentioned it to his father, probably bragged about it, in fact. The panicked mayor had then sent Tolliver scurrying straight to Oscar. Leroy's near revelation that his father was a big shot in the Aryan movement fit. The tight relationship between Delbert and Henry Lucas, whose case had been pending before Judge Price at the time of his death, jibed with her theory. There was no doubt in her mind that one of them was responsible not only for the judge's death, but for Dave's. It was entirely likely that it was a conspiracy among the whole damned bunch of them.

Inside the house, she called Oscar. "I think I know who's behind the skinheads and maybe even Judge Price's murder," she announced.

"Who?"

"I want to do one more interview before I say. Just tell me one thing. Has there ever been the slightest whisper of scandal around Delbert Reed? Does he have ties to the Klan?"

"Jesus, Amanda, you're not thinking of going after Delbert, are you? He's a little too slick and I've never much liked him, but the man's clean as a whistle. You know how the press goes after candidates for office these days."

"Not in some local mayor's race way out here," she countered. "But I'd bet he didn't realize what it would be like once he decided to run for the legislature. When he found out the media hounds would be after him, maybe he decided he'd better cover his tracks."

"I don't know," he said cautiously. "I want the people behind those skinheads in the worst way, but it seems to me you're leaping to some pretty dangerous conclusions.''

"Take a look at this week's *Gazette* and tell me if you think I've gone too far. The boy in that Reed family picture is the same one Ronnie arranged for me to meet. Do you expect me to believe that he's a skinhead leader and his father knows nothing about it?''

Oscar was silent for fully a minute. "I want to come with you when you talk to Delbert," he said, his voice strained. She could just envision him pummeling the mayor to a bloody pulp before she'd asked the first question.

"Oscar, that's not a good idea.''

"Neither is your going to see him alone. The man's about to run for the state legislature. If he has hidden his ties to the Klan all these years like you said, he's not going to want them exposed at this late date. That makes him dangerous.''

"I have a bodyguard looking out for me.''

She could hear the crash as the front legs of Oscar's chair hit the floor. "You do?''

"Provided by Miss Martha. She thinks I'm reckless.''

"Pretty good judge of character isn't she?''

"Thanks for your vote of confidence. I'll be in touch.''

She ran out of the house and headed straight to her car. She considered warning Carmody that she was heading out again, but she was certain he wouldn't dare lose her twice in one day. She noted that he was still parked discreetly under a stand of trees just to the left of the driveway. From that spot he had a clear view of the front and back of the house, as well as the access road. The car's tinted windows were rolled up tight.

Counting on him to follow, she took off, heading straight for the mayor's house at a speed designed to pick up the sheriff or his deputy along the way. Naturally, they were nowhere to be found when she needed them. At least she reached her destination about ten minutes faster than she had any legal right to.

Delbert's sprawling brick ranch-style house was tucked into a stand of trees atop a low rise. At least five acres of prime real estate lay spread out below. Even though it was nearing midnight, lights were still on in most of the rooms. Amanda approached the front door cautiously, still trying to decide on the best approach to take. Finally, she took a deep breath and knocked. She saw a shadow move across the front of the house, then the fluttering of the curtain as someone peered out. Then a young girl, no more than twelve, opened the door. With her hair in a sassy ponytail and freckles sprinkled lightly across her nose, there was no mistaking her as one of the daughters pictured in the paper. She regarded Amanda with frank curiosity.

"Hi! You're that reporter, aren't you? The one who got stood up at the altar." She blushed. "Sorry. That was probably rude of me, wasn't it? Mother's always saying I open my mouth before I think. Can I help you?"

Amanda couldn't help grinning back at her. "Actually, I was hoping to speak with your father. Is he around?"

"Are you kidding? Stay home, when he could be out rallying a couple of votes. No way. There's some kind of meeting in town."

Just then a voice called from inside, "Who is it, Linda?"

"It's Amanda Roberts, Mother. She's looking for Daddy. I told her he's in town."

"Do you know where the meeting is?" Amanda asked.

"Behind Lacey's I guess. That's where it usually is."

"Thanks," Amanda said, hurrying off before Mrs. Reed could decide to interfere.

She reached Lacey's in less than twenty minutes, again testing her speed against Eldon and Buford's fancy new radar. Apparently, they weren't out with it tonight. Maybe their fascination with the new toy had worn off. She hadn't actually seen Kenny's headlights in her rearview mirror either, but it was too late to worry about that now.

Amanda bounced into the crowded parking lot at Lacey's and found a space way back in a shadowy corner. Before getting out, she stopped to consider a plan. None came to her beyond peering in the back windows to see what was happening before she made her grand entrance.

Sticking to the shadows, she crossed the parking lot and came up behind the building. Unfortunately, all of the windows were up high. The only way she could see in would be to climb up on one of the garbage dumpsters. Grimacing at the prospect, she held her breath and boosted herself up. Standing on tiptoe, she was just able to see through the filthy glass. What she saw made the climb and withstanding the awful stench worthwhile.

One table was spread with pamphlets and buttons, which were definitely not ordinary campaign materials. Even from her distant vantage point she could pick out the racist phrases. Though she couldn't see him, she recognized the hesitant speech pattern of George Tolliver. Less familiar was the venom in his tone. He was exhorting this crowd of believers every bit as effectively as Seth Hawkins stirred his followers on a Sunday morning.

And then Delbert Reed began to speak. From the few words she could hear, he was not discussing the state of the economy. In front of this partisan crowd, he was hitting hard on the issues dearest to a racist's heart. Amanda was so excited, she almost slid from her perch. She had him. There was no way he could wriggle out of his connection to everything.

Or was there? Sure, she could blow his cover as a respectable politician, but what about hard evidence of criminal activity? Fingerprints? Access to the dynamite or the makings of the similar mail bomb? All she really had was speculation.

Deflated, she almost missed the murmur of discontent that was beginning to swell. A shouted taunt drew her attention back. Now that voices were being raised, she could hear just about everything.

"You're going soft, Delbert. You're turning into one of them nigger lovers, just like the rest of those fancy

politicians. You never did want folks to know your real
beliefs, did you? You hid out for years behind Tolliver,
but everyone hereabouts knew it was you pulling the
strings. Your hands are just as bloody as ours. There's
no hiding now."

"He's right," Tolliver said, moving swiftly to Delbert's
side. "Your boy's . . . Leroy's meeting up with that reporter has ruined your chances. She's probably linked us
all together by now. Face it, you'll have to pull out or
face exposure."

The mayor turned pale. "Not run? Are you out of
your mind?"

"It's the only way."

"Yeah, Pop," a familiar voice answered. "Too bad."

Delbert faced the back of the room. "*You?*"

Amanda couldn't see Leroy's face, but she recognized
the voice as he said, "The man said it all, Pop. You
were going soft. I woke up one day and found myself
living with a hypocrite for a daddy."

"I won't drop out of the race. I'll stop that article."

"How?" Leroy demanded, moving forward. "How
you gonna do that? Tolliver tried."

Delbert turned to the quartet in the front row. "Find
the Roberts woman and take care of it," he said, his
voice flat and cold.

Amanda's heart slammed against her chest as the
implications sank in. She had just listened to a man, a
prominent politician, order her execution. She had to get
away, get to someone in authority with what she knew
before it was too late, not just for her, but for Joe.

Perspiration ran down her back as she slid to the ground and began to run. She had taken no more than half a dozen steps when a hand clamped over her mouth. Her arm was pinned behind her at an angle so painful it made her cry out, although the sound was muffled. Kicking and clawing at her captor, she tried desperately to free herself, but he was too strong. Only when she bit down hard on his hand did he yelp softly.

"Dammit, Amanda, why couldn't you let well enough alone," Jeffrey Dunne said, a trace of genuine sorrow in his voice as he half pushed, half carried her away from Lacey's Bar and Grill.

Oh, hell, she thought wearily. This was definitely an angle she hadn't considered.

CHAPTER

Sixteen

*J*EFFREY Dunne loosened his grip and Amanda spun around furiously. She was relieved he wasn't one of those goons from inside, but she nevertheless doubted his integrity. She couldn't afford to trust anyone in the vicinity of Lacey's right now.

"What the hell do you think you're doing?" she demanded.

"Getting you out of here."

"I'm not going anywhere with you," she said, digging in her heels and wondering where the hell her bodyguard was.

"Really?"

"Not until you answer a few questions, starting with why you're manhandling me." For all she knew he was about to deliver her up to those bloodthirsty killers inside, who'd just whooped so enthusiastically at being given permission to kill her.

"I'll answer all of your questions later," he said. "Now."

He shook his head wearily, then picked her up like a rag doll and carried her the rest of the way to his car. When he plunked her down, she hit the ground so hard her teeth rattled.

"Do you honestly think you can fight me?" he asked.

From her humiliated vantage point, she studied his athletic build and the determination in his eyes and decided that only a well-directed kick had any hope at all of being effective. She put all the force at her command into the sudden move, only to have a hand whip out and grab her ankle. The next thing she knew she was flat on her back on the red clay parking lot, her whole body jarred by the impact. Dunne stood calmly over her. His lips quirked with infuriating amusement.

"It really is a shame you're so crazy about Donelli," he taunted. "I think you and I could have had a challenging relationship."

"You and I?" she said, tasting blood where she'd apparently bitten her lip in the fall. "In your dreams. Have you lost it entirely, Mr. Dunne?"

A surprising look of regret passed across his face. He held out his hand to help her up. Ignoring it, she rose with as much dignity as she could manage, brushing the dirt and gravel off her jeans.

He sighed and again she heard a faint, troubling hint of regret. It confused her. Something about this whole scene was out of kilter, but she couldn't pinpoint exactly what it was.

"Let's go," he said, that brisk command back in his voice.

"Would it do me any good to inquire where you're taking me?"

"Not a bit," he said cheerfully.

"You really are a nasty, despicable, sadistic creep, aren't you?" she said, trying the description out. It didn't ring true and she found herself unable to muster up much enthusiasm for it.

"You really shouldn't listen to everything Jim Harrison tells you."

"The comment was based on my own observation."

"Then you aren't nearly the reporter I thought you were," he said, tucking her into his car with exaggerated chivalry and locking the door securely. She noted that as in most police cars there was no way for her to unlock it. Since it appeared unlikely to fall open accidentally either, she leaned against it and nursed her tender elbow, which had a dandy bruise from its contact with the ground. Whenever Dunne glanced over to check on her, she glared at him. He seemed to find the minor rebellion amusing.

As they sped along Route 20 toward Atlanta, Amanda tried to make sense of Dunne kidnapping her. Despite the fact that he'd insisted she come with him, she had the distinct impression that he wasn't really out to do her any particular harm. He'd seemed more put out than menacing.

"Are you kidnapping me?" she inquired finally.

"In a manner of speaking."

She fell silent again and studied him. He seemed every

bit as relaxed as if they were merely going for an evening drive for ice cream. Weren't kidnappers supposed to be tense?

"I don't get it," she said finally. "Are you in this with them?"

"Them?"

"Reed and Lucas. Reed's son. George Tolliver, too, I guess."

"Just what is it they're into?" he said cautiously.

"The Klan. Skinheads. Terrorism. Murder."

He shook his head. "I have to hand it to you, Amanda. You've put it all together. You're every bit as good as Donelli said you were."

Her head snapped around at that. "When did you talk to Joe?"

His eyes widened innocently. "Did I say I'd talked to him?"

"You quoted him. You said, and now I'm quoting, 'You're every bit as good as Donelli said you were.'"

"Yep. That's reasonably accurate."

"It's damned accurate and it fits with what I discovered earlier."

"Which was?"

"That Joe had been calling FBI headquarters. I assumed Dave was his contact. Maybe it was you. Am I right?"

Since it seemed unlikely that he would give her a straight answer, she watched closely for some faint flicker in his expressive eyes that would be tantamount to an admission. For once those eyes remained studiously blank.

"Are you going to answer me or not?" she snapped.

"Not."

Amanda muttered a particularly nasty description of his parentage. "What I still can't figure out," she said, when he didn't react to her comment, "is where you fit into all this."

"Me? I'm the good guy, remember."

"So I thought, until you came up behind me, practically mugged me, and kidnapped me."

"I wish you'd stop saying that."

"What?"

"About the kidnapping. It's bad for my law-abiding image."

"But you admitted it."

"Bad reporting, Amanda. I said—and I quote—*in a manner of speaking*."

"Okay, then you put a label on my unwilling presence in this car."

"Protective custody."

"An interesting concept. I felt safer a few hours ago, though."

"Does that mean you missed what went on in that room tonight right before you dashed into my waiting arms?"

"No," she said cautiously. "Which part are you talking about?"

"I believe their precise words—which we have on a tape we were able to set up earlier, of course—were '*Find the Roberts woman and take care of it.*' They weren't consenting to an interview."

Dunne's reference to bugging the room reassured her

somewhat. It suggested his allegiance was where it ought to be. She sighed. "Now that you have what you need on them, can't you just bring them in?"

"Not quite yet. It would be helpful if they'd make a move."

A niggling little suspicion wormed its way into her gut. "On me?"

He had the grace to look guilty. "Well, it would help. One last nail in the coffin, so to speak."

"Do you really think they'll come after me? Maybe it was just macho talk," she suggested hopefully.

"It's not macho until they've nailed your hide. Besides, you're a real danger to them. You've been busy linking them together like some damned daisy chain. If your story actually hit the newsstands, it would put a serious dent in their respectability."

"Respectability? They're a bunch of lowdown terrorists."

"An unflattering description they would rather not have publicized, especially Delbert. He's worked so hard to keep his squeaky clean image these last few years."

Amanda's gaze narrowed. She decided to put the FBI's sudden chivalry to the test. "So, you're calling this a simple rescue?"

"Exactly."

"Then you won't mind if I just say thanks, but no thanks. I'll take care of myself," she said as he rolled to a stop in front of a nondescript apartment complex, one of those rabbit warrens that filled acres of land with brick sameness.

"Your bodyguard was no match for them. What makes you think you are?"

"They got to Ken?"

"He's in the hospital. He was beaten up and dragged off into the bushes, courtesy of a few playful skinheads. Didn't you wonder why he hadn't followed you?"

"Yes, but . . ."

"But you were too anxious to get your story to check it out."

She winced. "Is he okay?"

"He will be. Now are you convinced that I'm doing this for your own good?"

Not quite ready to go that far, she said, "I have a gun back at Donelli's. I know how to use it."

"But why bother, when you're perfectly safe here for the moment," he said pleasantly. He held open the door. "Now come along."

Since his hand was clamped firmly around her sore elbow again, she abandoned her immediate escape plans. "There'd better be a phone in this place," she said. "I want to call my attorney and complain about the tactics the FBI uses against innocent citizens."

"Not likely," he muttered.

She retreated into silence as he prodded her along the sidewalk toward an entrance to a small four-unit building. In the foyer, she glanced at the names on the mailboxes, hoping to see one she'd recognize. Two were neatly typed and unfamiliar. One was smudged. The fourth was missing. Naturally, that was the apartment to which Dunne led her. Despite what Dunne had told her, she was still feeling a lot more like the FBI's victim than Delbert Reed's.

Dunne tapped on the door. Amanda could hear footsteps crossing the wooden floor, then the subtle stillness that suggested they were being observed through the peephole. Several locks were turned and the door swung open. The man inside, the same one who'd been on guard at Donelli's after the car bombing, nodded at Dunne, then moved aside.

Amanda took one step into the apartment and realized that someone was standing in the shadows. She felt her whole body tense.

"It took you long enough to get here."

At the sound of that Brooklyn accent, that wry amusement, Amanda went absolutely still. Only one person she knew in these parts could make her heart trip with that precise combination: Donelli.

"Joe," she whispered hesitantly, afraid to believe the worst nightmare of her life was finally over, straining her eyes for a first glimpse of him. Still feeling as though the wind had been knocked out of her, she took another step, then another. Familiar arms wrapped around her, crushing her to familiar warmth. Tears streamed down her face as she clung to him. A shudder sighed through him.

"Oh, God, I've missed you," she murmured against his chest. "I've been so scared. Why didn't you call? Are you okay? What are you doing here? Have you been here the whole time or did the FBI rescue you?" She whirled on Dunne. "Why didn't you tell me he was here?"

"Whoa. Slow down," Donelli said. "One question at a time." He looked pointedly at Dunne and the other man. "Could we have a little privacy, please?"

Dunne grinned. "Why not? I have some arrests to make tonight anyway."

Amanda's gaze shot to Dunne. "Arrests?"

Donelli shook his head, his expression regretful. "You've said the magic word, Jeff. Notice how quickly she's lost interest in me?"

"Not so," she said, her arm going around his waist. "I'm not about to let you out of my sight ever again. Still . . ."

"Here it comes," Joe said.

"No, you may not come along," Dunne said.

"But that's obstruction of the media or something."

"Sue me."

"I will," she vowed. "Besides, I thought you wanted them to make a move on me."

"We have Donelli's staked out, just waiting for them to show up."

Donelli pressed his lips to the back of her neck. "Perhaps I can find some way to keep you distracted until Jeffrey comes back with a report."

"I don't want a report, dammit. I want to be there. Are you going after Tolliver or Lucas or Reed or all three of them? Is this for Dave's murder or for Judge Price's?"

Joe looked resigned. "She'll make our lives miserable if you don't let her go along."

"I don't like it," Dunne said. "I want this strictly by the book. I don't want these guys screaming that we violated their rights, denied them the possibility of a fair trial, all that sort of garbage. It's taken us years to get all of them, plus our tape recorder, in the same room at the same time, so we could make the conspiracy charges stick.''

"Whose rights are you worried about?" Amanda demanded. "Will you two cut to the chase and tell me what's going down tonight?"

"Delbert Reed's empire is about to come tumbling down, thanks to you, Amanda. You should be congratulating yourself."

"What exactly did I do?" she said slowly.

"Something the rest of us couldn't do. You went charging after Joe's kidnapper like an avenging angel. Delbert and his pals got scared. They insisted on a meeting tonight. Then they told him they wanted him to forget about running for the legislature. They figured that would take the heat off."

"That's awfully naive."

"For the most part, these aren't sophisticated criminals. They're sneaky weasels, who like to hit under cover of darkness. Judge Price's murder wasn't like some calculated mob slaying. It was an unthought-out, desperate act by some men who thought they could protect their chosen leader, Delbert."

"And killing me?"

"You heard him. That was Delbert's suggested alternative to backing out of the race."

Amanda shivered. "Why the hell didn't you arrest them long before this?"

''We never had the hard evidence, not until Dave came in here undercover on that skinhead operation. We needed to get somebody on the inside. He was able to link those kids with the Klan and tied the whole bunch of them to Delbert, but even then we didn't have the bomber. Finding that dynamite in Jeeter's shed was our first big break. Everything in that sack tied to the two previous bombings.''

''He was the bomber, then?''

''No. The dynamite was planted there by one of the skinheads to make it look as though he was.''

''How do you know that?''

''An informant. Dave was able to get one of the kids to turn state's evidence.''

''Ronnie?''

He shook his head. ''No. Delbert's son.''

''Leroy turned informant?'' Amanda was incredulous. ''Why?''

''To embarrass his hypocritical father, to hear him tell it. I'm not sure if he really got sick of all the rhetoric or if he was just mad because Daddy wouldn't increase his allowance. Who can tell with a kid that age? At any rate, between his information and you stirring things up, we got them to start making mistakes. Setting up Jeeter was their first one.

''They were willing to sacrifice him. They also figured he'd be less dangerous to them behind bars. Unfortunately for them, it just made him mad as hell. He started talking. He knows quite a lot.''

Amanda recalled him bragging that Delbert needed

him. Apparently, what the mayor had really needed from Jeeter was his silence. "Didn't they know he'd start talking?"

"My guess is they figured no one would believe an old drunk over all these well-respected town leaders. Today, when you refused to back off of that story, it all started unraveling."

"And before today?" Amanda said slowly. She stepped away from Joe and looked into his eyes. She saw the familiar love, but she also saw a faint shadow of guilt. "You were never kidnapped, were you?"

"No."

"Have you been working with them from the beginning? Did you move down here to be a part of this investigation?"

"No. I didn't even know Dave was here until I tracked him down to tell him about the wedding. Even then, he never said exactly what he was working on. I didn't figure it out until I started looking into the skinhead thing for Megan Reardon."

Suddenly, Amanda didn't like the way this was adding up. "But Megan hasn't been your boss for awhile now has she? You've been working for the goddamned FBI."

"No. I only called them to see what they knew about the skinheads. I stumbled right into the thick of the investigation."

"And you couldn't tell me about it?"

"Amanda, you know all about client confidentiality. Top that with the danger I could have been putting Dave in, if I'd told you what was going on."

"I'm not the one who got him killed, though, am I?" she said furiously. "That was just an innocent bunch of boys playing hide-and-seek with the bad guys, no girls allowed. Am I getting warm?"

"Absolutely not," Dunne said, though the dull red in his cheeks said otherwise.

"Don't even try that, Jeff. She'll never buy into it. It was the only way, Amanda," Joe said reasonably. "You're a reporter. If I'd told you what was going on, it would have compromised everything."

"Believe me, he tried to talk us into bringing you in on it," Dunne said hurriedly. "Especially after the bombing."

"Endlessly," the other FBI agent confirmed.

Amanda was not appeased. "So, you backed them into a corner and waited for something to break, is that right? With all these hotshot investigators on the case, why weren't you able to prevent the bombing that killed Dave?"

"It happened too quickly. We didn't realize his cover'd been blown until it was too late."

"Who blew it?"

"Ronnie Reardon. I doubt he meant to, but he told one of them that Dave was going to be my best man. They knew someone had been leaking information and pinned it on him. I think they were hoping to get both of us in that blast. If I hadn't gone back inside to get the wedding ring, they would have."

"Once the car blew up, you called the FBI and they took over from there."

"Right," Dunne said. "We brought Joe here and waited."

"Knowing I'd go off half-cocked to try to solve the killing and find Joe? You set me up! You've been having me followed from the beginning, hoping I'd stumble on the truth or lure them into making a mistake, right? Delbert wasn't scared of you. You hadn't been able to pin the Price murder on him in all this time. He had no reason to figure you would now. I was the real threat, along with his son, because we could expose his Klan ties. Am I getting warm?"

All three men had the grace to look embarrassed. "How dare you? I'm not a goddamned pawn to be manipulated," she shouted at Dunne.

The worst of it, though, wasn't that the FBI had used her. She supposed they could come up with all sorts of justification for using whatever weapons they could to break open the case. It was Donelli's role in all of this that sickened her.

At some signal that she apparently missed, Dunne and the other FBI agent slipped from the room, leaving her alone with Joe.

"How could you?" she said softly, still shaken by the awful emptiness she felt.

She saw the stubborn glint in his eyes, the refusal to accept the guilt she was heaping on him. She recognized that expression. She'd seen it often enough when cops were justifying their actions. And, though he'd been fighting against it for a long time now, at heart Donelli was still a cop.

"I had no choice, Amanda. Dave and I go back a long way. I knew the FBI would never let any harm come to you and I knew you were good enough to accomplish what they needed. Once you stop and think about what you've pulled off, you'll see how important it was. It's the biggest case in these parts in years."

"Any means to an end," she said bitterly. "That's the FBI, all right."

"And any good journalist," he countered. "You bend the rules all the time."

Amanda winced, unable to think of an adequate defense to that.

His brown eyes met hers. "Are you going to forgive me?"

She shook her head. "It's not that easy. For days now I've been terrified that I'd lost you. You let me go through that kind of agony. No, worse that that. You deliberately put me through it."

"I am sorry for that, but I couldn't see any other way to wrap this up quickly. I owed Dave."

"Why? Because you used to play football with him?"

"No, because he blew his cover by being connected with me. I was responsible for his death, Amanda. There was no way I could walk away from what had to be done after that. Can't you see that? I owed him."

Actually, she could. She knew all about his sense of duty, his ethics. Loyalty and old ties meant everything to a man like Joe. She wanted to believe that he'd prove that same kind of loyalty to her, if it came down to it, but right now she simply felt hurt and angry. She couldn't even relish the triumph of solving the case, of getting the hard-hitting story she'd gone after, of bringing down what might be the last bastion of hatemongers around here. Joe apparently sensed the uncertainty that she was only beginning to acknowledge.

"I hear the church is available again on Saturday," he said. "Jeff tells me you looked beautiful in your wedding dress. Any chance I could get to see for myself?"

One of these days the anger and hurt would fade and she would be proud of the principles of this man who saw things so clearly in terms of right and wrong. Now, though, it was still far too soon.

She slipped her hand into his and held on tight. "I don't think so. Not right now, anyway."

He nodded, his eyes filled with pain and acceptance. "I guess I understand how you feel."

"If you do, if you really do," she said, searching his face for the truth, "then maybe someday we'll have another chance."

He pulled her close. "I guess I'll just have to do my damnedest to earn that right."

She knew deep down that he'd try, too. Now, though, it was all too much for her. "I don't suppose I could talk you into going after Jeffrey Dunne, could I?"

He grinned. "He'll probably ring my neck, but I guess you have every right to be in on the kill. They should be swarming all over our house and Lacey's by now."

The prospect didn't make her attitude toward the bunch of them any more mellow, but it definitely cheered her up. She rather liked the idea of seeing the mayor behind bars in that pitiful little jail cell of Eldon's, though it was far more likely that the FBI had a more secure place in mind.

Still, as she rode with Donelli back to Lacey's Bar and Grill and began drafting the opening line of her next article for *Inside Atlanta,* she couldn't help thinking that maybe this wouldn't turn out to be the lousiest week of her life after all.